Look With the Heart

"Surely there must be a cottage in the village in which you could stay?" the stranger suggested, invisible in the shadows.

"In the village?" Erlina echoed. "The . . . village . . . is dead!"

She paused for a moment and then continued.

"It has died because the . . . wicked . . . cruel . . . evil . . . Marquis murdered it!"

There was a long silence while the man in the shadows did not speak.

Erlina looked towards the darker part of the room.

She could vaguely see there was someone sitting in one of the armchairs in front of the fireplace.

"Wh-who are . . . you . . . ? . . . Is it possible . . ." she stammered, "can it be . . . true that you are . . . ?"

" . . . the wicked Marquis!" the stranger finished.

A Camfield Novel of Love by Barbara Cartland

"Barbara Cartland's novels are all distinguished by their intelligence, good sense, and good nature. . . ."
—ROMANTIC TIMES

"Who could give better advice on how to keep your romance going strong than the world's most famous romance novelist, Barbara Cartland?"
—THE STAR

Camfield Place,
Hatfield
Hertfordshire,
England

Dearest Reader,

Camfield Novels of Love mark a very exciting era of my books with Jove. They have already published nearly two hundred of my titles since they became my first publisher in America, and now all my original paperback romances in the future will be published exclusively by them.

As you already know, Camfield Place in Hertfordshire is my home, which originally existed in 1275, but was rebuilt in 1867 by the grandfather of Beatrix Potter.

It was here in this lovely house, with the best view in the county, that she wrote *The Tale of Peter Rabbit*. Mr. McGregor's garden is exactly as she described it. The door in the wall that the fat little rabbit could not squeeze underneath and the goldfish pool where the white cat sat twitching its tail are still there.

I had Camfield Place blessed when I came here in 1950 and was so happy with my husband until he died, and now with my children and grandchildren, that I know the atmosphere is filled with love and we have all been very lucky.

It is easy here to write of love and I know you will enjoy the Camfield Novels of Love. Their plots are definitely exciting and the covers very romantic. They come to you, like all my books, with love.

Bless you,

CAMFIELD NOVELS OF LOVE

by Barbara Cartland

THE POOR GOVERNESS
WINGED VICTORY
LUCKY IN LOVE
LOVE AND THE MARQUIS
A MIRACLE IN MUSIC
LIGHT OF THE GODS
BRIDE TO A BRIGAND
LOVE COMES WEST
A WITCH'S SPELL
SECRETS
THE STORMS OF LOVE
MOONLIGHT ON THE
  SPHINX
WHITE LILAC
REVENGE OF THE HEART
THE ISLAND OF LOVE
THERESA AND A TIGER
LOVE IS HEAVEN
MIRACLE FOR A MADONNA
A VERY UNUSUAL WIFE
THE PERIL AND THE
  PRINCE
ALONE AND AFRAID
TEMPTATION OF A
  TEACHER
ROYAL PUNISHMENT
THE DEVILISH DECEPTION
PARADISE FOUND
LOVE IS A GAMBLE
A VICTORY FOR LOVE
LOOK WITH LOVE
NEVER FORGET LOVE
HELGA IN HIDING
SAFE AT LAST
HAUNTED
CROWNED WITH LOVE
ESCAPE
THE DEVIL DEFEATED
THE SECRET OF THE
  MOSQUE
A DREAM IN SPAIN
THE LOVE TRAP
LISTEN TO LOVE
THE GOLDEN CAGE
LOVE CASTS OUT FEAR

A WORLD OF LOVE
DANCING ON A RAINBOW
LOVE JOINS THE CLANS
AN ANGEL RUNS AWAY
FORCED TO MARRY
BEWILDERED IN BERLIN
WANTED—A WEDDING RING
THE EARL ESCAPES
STARLIGHT OVER TUNIS
THE LOVE PUZZLE
LOVE AND KISSES
SAPPHIRES IN SIAM
A CARETAKER OF LOVE
SECRETS OF THE HEART
RIDING IN THE SKY
LOVERS IN LISBON
LOVE IS INVINCIBLE
THE GODDESS OF LOVE
AN ADVENTURE OF LOVE
THE HERB FOR HAPPINESS
ONLY A DREAM
SAVED BY LOVE
LITTLE TONGUES OF FIRE
A CHIEFTAIN FINDS LOVE
A LOVELY LIAR
THE PERFUME OF THE GODS
A KNIGHT IN PARIS
REVENGE IS SWEET
THE PASSIONATE PRINCESS
SOLITA AND THE SPIES
THE PERFECT PEARL
LOVE IS A MAZE
A CIRCUS FOR LOVE
THE TEMPLE OF LOVE
THE BARGAIN BRIDE
THE HAUNTED HEART
REAL LOVE OR FAKE
KISS FROM A STRANGER
A VERY SPECIAL LOVE
THE NECKLACE OF LOVE
A REVOLUTION OF LOVE
THE MARQUIS WINS
LOVE IS THE KEY
LOVE AT FIRST SIGHT
THE TAMING OF A TIGRESS

PARADISE IN PENANG
THE EARL RINGS A BELLE
THE QUEEN SAVES THE
  KING
NO DISGUISE FOR LOVE
LOVE LIFTS THE CURSE
BEAUTY OR BRAINS?
TOO PRECIOUS TO LOSE
HIDING
A TANGLED WEB
JUST FATE
A MIRACLE IN MEXICO
WARNED BY A GHOST
TWO HEARTS IN HUNGARY
A THEATER OF LOVE
A DYNASTY OF LOVE
MAGIC FROM THE HEART
THE WINDMILL OF LOVE
LOVE STRIKES A DEVIL
LOVE AND WAR
SEEK THE STARS
A CORONATION OF LOVE
A WISH COMES TRUE
LOVED FOR HIMSELF
A KISS IN ROME
HIDDEN BY LOVE
BORN OF LOVE
WALKING TO
  WONDERLAND
TERROR FROM THE
  THRONE
THE CAVE OF LOVE
THE PEAKS OF ECSTASY
LUCKY LOGAN FINDS LOVE
THE ANGEL AND THE
  RAKE
THE QUEEN OF HEARTS
THE WICKED WIDOW
TO SCOTLAND AND LOVE
LOVE AT THE RITZ
THE DANGEROUS
  MARRIAGE
GOOD OR BAD?
THIS IS LOVE
RUNNING AWAY TO LOVE

A NEW CAMFIELD NOVEL OF LOVE BY

BARBARA CARTLAND

Look With the Heart

JOVE BOOKS, NEW YORK

LOOK WITH THE HEART

A Jove Book / published by arrangement with
the author

PRINTING HISTORY
Jove edition / March 1994

ISBN: 0-515-11341-7

A JOVE BOOK®
Jove Books are published by The Berkley Publishing Group,
200 Madison Avenue, New York, New York 10016.
JOVE and the "J" design are trademarks belonging to
Jove Publications, Inc.

PRINTED IN THE UNITED STATES OF AMERICA

10 9 8 7 6 5 4 3 2 1

Author's Note

IN my travels all over the world I have met a great many Healers. When I was at the foot of the Himalayas, I talked to one who was 160 years old in the woods in Nepal.

There were others beside the Ganges, one near the Diamond Mines in Hyderabad, and another in the exquisitely beautiful Lake Palace at Udaipur.

They, all of them, tried to give the Light Force through their hands or their concentration to the person who needed their help.

In this country, the two Healers I found who work in the same way (believing in the Light that comes from God) are Princess Helena Moutafian, and Joseph Corvo. Corvo is a genius and works on his patients with Zone Therapy.

Fennel was believed to have a great effect

on the eyes from the time of the Greeks, who not only believed in its effectiveness in healing eyes, but also used it during their Olympic Games as a wreath to put round the head of the Victor.

Look With the Heart

chapter one

1819

ERLINA Sherwood stood looking helplessly as the
flames soared higher and higher.

She could hardly believe that her home was
being irretrievably destroyed.

There was a resounding crash as part of the
roof fell in. She felt her brother's hand slip into
hers.

"I do not think we can save any more," he said.

"No, we must ... not go near ... it again,"
Erlina managed to say.

They were able to save a small number of
chairs and pictures, which she and Gerry, who
was eleven, had managed to pull out of the
hall.

As it was in the middle of the night and they
were some distance from the village, no-one had
come to help them.

The old servants, Dawes and his wife, could only stand staring at the flames, weeping.

It was in fact Dawes who had caused the fire.

He had got out of bed in the night and the candle he had left burning by his bedside had toppled over onto the bed.

He did not realise at first that the bed-clothes were burning.

When he did, he tried to put out the fire himself.

When the blaze became too strong for him to cope with, his wife ran screaming out of the back door.

It was only then that he hurried through the house to wake Erlina.

He told her what had happened and that it was his fault.

Erlina quickly woke her brother, who was in the next room.

They pulled on some clothes and ran downstairs.

By this time, the flames were completely out of control.

Sherwood House was very old, in fact, it had been built in Tudor times.

The wooden beams and floors were dry and quickly caught fire.

Erlina and Gerry managed to bring only half-a-dozen pieces out through the front-door into the garden.

The flames were destroying everything she knew and loved.

Another part of the roof fell.

Then there was just the crackle of the flames,

with the skeleton of the walls silhouetted against them.

"What are we going to do?" Gerry asked.

It was a question which Erlina was already asking herself.

She knew she had to think for the two old servants also.

"We will have to drive into the village," she said. "Thank goodness the horses are safe."

Fortunately, the stables were built some distance from the house.

It was obvious that the flames would not reach them.

"What shall we do about the Daweses?" Gerry asked.

"We will take them with us," Erlina said. "Go and put *Nobby* between the shafts of the pony-cart."

Gerry ran off.

He was young, but he was a sensible and helpful little boy.

Erlina walked towards the old couple.

" 'Tis terrible . . . terrible!" the old woman was sobbing. "Everything's bin burnt—everything!"

Her voice was almost incoherent.

Erlina could do nothing but pat her shoulder.

"We have to be brave," she said.

" 'T'were m'fault, Miss," Dawes said. "There's no one t'blame but me!"

"It is something that might have happened at any time," Erlina said consolingly. "The house is so old that I think I always knew that if there was a fire, nothing could save it."

Mrs. Dawes was still sobbing, and the tears

were running down the old man's cheeks.

Erlina felt like crying herself, but she knew it would do no good.

"I have sent Master Gerry to fetch the pony-cart," she said. "We will drive into the village and ask the Vicar if we can stay with him for the rest of the night."

She did not wait to hear what the Daweses had to say, but walked off towards the stables, knowing she must help Gerry.

He already had *Nobby,* who was a reliable old pony, out of his stall.

She helped Gerry fit him between the shafts.

The pony-cart was old, like everything else they possessed.

She thought, despairingly, that unless they lay down on the straw with the horses they would not have a roof over their heads.

"Have you fastened the shaft on your side?" she asked Gerry.

"I think it is all right," he answered. "It is difficult to see in the dark."

There were stars overhead, but no moon.

Erlina knew, however, that *Nobby* would find his way to the Vicarage without any trouble.

She got into the pony-cart and picked up the reins.

Then, as Gerry would have joined her, she said:

"Shut the door of the stable. We do not want the horses let out to-morrow if people come up to look at the fire."

"I do not suppose they will want to walk so far," Gerry answered, "except, of course, for the Vicar and his family."

Erlina did not answer.

She only waited while he closed the stable-door and pushed the bolt into place.

Gerry climbed into the pony cart.

Erlina drove carefully out from the stables and down the cobbled way to the front of the house.

The Daweses were waiting where she had left them, but there was now even less of the house standing than there had been before.

She could not bear to look at it.

She did not want to know that everything she possessed, including her clothes, would soon be nothing but ashes.

All that was left was the small number of things which she and Gerry had rescued, lying on the grass some way from the fire.

She wished they had had time to bring the pictures of their ancestors from the Dining-Room.

She had always loved the one of her Father, who had been the fifth Baronet. Gerry was now the sixth.

Erlina pulled the pony-cart to a standstill.

She told Mr. and Mrs. Dawes to climb in.

Gerry got out so that Mrs. Dawes could get in first.

She was still crying, and Erlina tried to think of something comforting to say, but the words would not come to her lips.

Gerry told Dawes to sit beside his wife, and he sat next to Erlina.

They went down the drive.

Erlina did not look back at the blazing building silhouetted against the dark foliage of the trees behind it.

She could, however, hear the crackle of the flames. A faint breeze was blowing burning cinders over the lawn.

Then there was only the clip-clop of *Nobby*'s hooves on the drive.

When they reached the gates, the fire was out of their sight.

There were only the stars overhead, and when they reached it, the darkness of the village with its empty ruined cottages.

Erlina drove on until they came to the grey Norman Church where she had been christened and later confirmed.

Her Mother and Father were buried in the Churchyard in the family vault.

It contained all the previous members of the family who had lived in Sherwood House since it was first built.

The Vicarage, which was beside the Church, was only about a hundred years old.

The window-frames and doors were badly in need of paint.

As Erlina knew, there was a hole in the roof which had not been repaired.

Gerry got out and raised the knocker on the front door.

He knocked twice before a window opened and the Vicar put out his head.

"Who is it?" he asked. "What do you want?"

"It is me, Erlina Sherwood. Our house is on fire, and as we have nowhere to go, we have come to you."

"Goodness gracious!" the Reverend Piran Garnet exclaimed. "I will come down."

It took some minutes for him to dress before he opened the front-door.

The Vicar, a middle-aged man, had always been respected and loved by his Parishioners, few as there now were remaining.

As he saw Gerry waiting for him on the doorstep, he put his arm round the boy and pulled him close.

"What has happened, Gerry?" he asked.

"The house caught fire, Vicar," Gerry answered, "and already there is almost nothing left—nothing at all!"

Erlina thought afterwards that it was characteristic of the Vicar to have taken everything in his stride.

He sent the Daweses to the Kitchen and told them to make some coffee for Erlina and themselves.

He then found some cider for Gerry to drink.

After *Nobby* had been put in the stable, they went into the Sitting-Room.

"It was Dawes who accidentally started the fire," Erlina explained, "and he is terribly upset about it. But once the flames had got a hold, there was nothing anybody could have done to stop it."

"I can understand that," the Vicar said. "I will go up first thing in the morning to see if any of the furniture can be saved."

Erlina shook her head.

"There is no chance of that. Gerry and I managed to carry a few things out of the hall, but it was too dangerous to attempt to rescue anything from any of the rooms."

7

The Vicar wisely did not let them talk for long.

He took them upstairs and told Gerry to get into bed with one of his two sons.

By taking his daughter into bed with him and his wife, he provided Erlina with a bed.

She knew only too well that there were no habitable rooms on the top floor, as the roof leaked.

There was no one left in the village to do the repairs, even if the Vicar had been able to pay for them.

Before Erlina fell asleep from sheer exhaustion, she wondered despairingly where she and Gerry could go.

How would they be able to live in the future?

"Please God . . . help us," she prayed, "please . . . please."

*   *   *

When Erlina, with dark lines under her eyes, came down to breakfast, she found Gerry already seated at the table.

The Vicar's children were also there.

Mrs. Garnet was bringing in their breakfast from the Kitchen.

She put the plates down in front of the children before kissing Erlina.

"I am sorry," she said, "more sorry than I can possibly say. How can such a dreadful thing have happened?"

"I have already spoken to old Henry," the Vicar said. "He saw the fire through the trees last night and walked up at dawn to see what had happened."

"That was kind of him," Erlina remarked, knowing that Henry was an old man who found it difficult to walk far.

"I am afraid he came back with bad news," the Vicar continued. "The fire is subsiding simply because there is nothing left to burn."

It was only what Erlina expected.

At the same time, she felt it was like a dagger-thrust in her breast.

"Henry gave the horses water and some food," the Vicar went on, "and said the chickens were all right."

Erlina could not even smile her thanks.

"Now, do not start worrying until you have had some breakfast," Mrs. Garnet said. "Thank Heaven, we have hens, otherwise we would be starving to death like everyone else who is left in this benighted place!"

As she finished speaking, she walked back into the Kitchen.

Erlina looked at the Vicar.

"Have you heard anything from the Marquis?" she asked in a low voice.

The Vicar shook his head.

"We are living only on what the Bishop sends me out of charity," he replied. "He has written to His Lordship, but there has been no reply."

"I cannot believe it!" Erlina cried. "How can he behave in this appalling manner to you, as well as to everybody else in the Parish?"

"I cannot understand it myself," the Vicar agreed, "and Meldon Hall is becoming almost as dilapidated as we are!"

There was no need to say anything.

Erlina had talked and talked about the dreadful

conditions in which they were all living.

There were no words left with which to describe the behaviour of the Marquis of Meldon.

When the old Marquis had died five years ago, his son had come into the title and the large Estate. Everyone had expected things to go on as they always had.

It had only been a question of when the new Marquis would come home.

He would, they thought, organise the lives of the villagers as his Father and Grandfather had done before him.

Practically every man and woman worked in some capacity on the Estate or in the "Big House."

After six months had passed without any sign of the new Marquis, everybody began to be apprehensive.

They asked nervously what was going on.

Mr. Cranley, who had been in charge of the house and the Estate for years, began to give the workers notice to leave.

"What's 'appening? Why be us sent away?" they asked indignantly.

Because it was traditional, their Fathers, their Grandfathers and their Great-Grandfathers had all worked at Meldon.

It was all very difficult for Mr. Cranley, who was a kindly man.

He had to explain that the new Marquis had no intention of spending any money on his Estate.

He also would not keep servants in a house which he did not intend to visit.

"But why? Why?" everybody asked.

Mr. Cranley could give them no explanation.

Then, as a year passed, then another, all the able men had left the village.

They had to get work elsewhere to keep themselves and their wives.

What was more, the cottages which needed repair began to fall down.

Finally, after five years, there was hardly anyone left in the village except for four men who worked for Sir Richard Sherwood.

Then they, too, began to leave.

" 'Tis like this, Miss," they explained to Erlina. "Our friends 'ave gone and there be nowhere in th' village now th' Inn's closed where us can even 'ave a drink."

"I know that," Erlina replied, "but we need you. How can we work our land if you are not there?"

"Us understands yer feelings, Miss," one man said, "but th' Missus says 'er's not walkin' two miles for a shop."

There was nothing Erlina could say.

She had wished despairingly that her Father were well enough to remonstrate the men.

But Sir Richard was a dying man.

When he did die, she was left with Gerry to look after and the Daweses who had nowhere else to go.

They stayed on in the house Erlina loved, which had always been her home.

It was heart-breaking to see the garden going to rack and ruin, to realise that their three-hundred acres of land was now growing nothing but weeds!

It meant, too, that she and Gerry had very little income.

Now that he was eleven, she knew that in a

year's time he ought to be going to Eton.

It was where their Father had been educated.

She would lie awake night after night, wondering what she could do.

Then in the morning she would struggle to keep the house clean.

She had to drive nearly two miles to buy the small amount of food they could afford.

She kept asking herself how they could go on like this, but could not find an answer.

The Garnets at the Vicarage were the only people to whom she could talk.

But they could find no solution for their own problems, let alone those of anybody else.

Every time Erlina drove through the village and saw the abandoned cottages and their weed-filled gardens she hated the Marquis more and more.

It was impossible to tell him what she felt.

He had not deigned even to answer the letters written to him by the Vicar.

It was Mrs. Garnet who was most voluble about it.

"The man is a murderer, that is what he is!" she said when she and Erlina were alone. "I know that the old people would have lived longer if they had had their pensions, and if my husband did not get a pittance from the Bishop, we too would starve to death!"

"Surely something can be done?" Erlina asked.

"My husband thought of going to London and speaking to the Marquis himself," Mrs. Garnet said. "But it would be very expensive, and I doubt if His Lordship would trouble himself to see him!"

"Why is he behaving like this?" Erlina enquired.

"That is what we are all asking," Mrs. Garnet replied. "There is plenty written in the newspapers about him enjoying himself, racing his horses at Newmarket, hunting in Leicestershire, and attending parties given by the Prince Regent, which cost thousands and thousands of pounds!"

Erlina knew that Mrs. Garnet had a sister who lived in London and sent her the newspapers from time to time.

This was why she knew so much about the Marquis's movements.

The more Erlina heard about him, the more she felt that he must be growing horns like the Devil.

He obviously never gave a thought to the people who had always depended upon his family for employment.

"I hate him! I hate him!" she would say night after night.

But she was quite certain that however violent her feelings were, they would not disturb the wicked Marquis.

Now, as Mrs. Garnet came back to the breakfast-table to put a poached egg in front of Erlina, she said to her husband:

"Have you thought of where Erlina and Gerry can go? Much as we love them, you know, Piran, there is no room fit for them to stay here."

"I am aware of that," the Vicar said quietly, "and there is only one place they can go."

"Where can that be?" Erlina asked.

She did not believe he could be clever enough to find somewhere suitable.

"Mr. Cranley must accommodate them at the Hall," the Vicar said.

If he had dropped a bomb on the table, Erlina could not have been more surprised.

"Do you mean—Meldon Hall?" she gasped.

"Why not? As you are well aware, there is really nowhere else," the Vicar said. "There is not a cottage in the village that does not leak, and while we would love to have you, you know yourself there is no room here unless you sleep on the floor."

"I think that is a very sensible suggestion," Mrs. Garnet said. "After all, Mr. Cranley is alone in that big house, as he has been for the last five years. He has had to look after himself since Lucy died."

Lucy had been the last remaining servant, Erlina knew, who had stayed on at the Hall after all the other servants had been given notice.

She was crippled with arthritis and had no relatives, and nowhere else to go.

She had been the Marquis's Nursery Maid when he was a small boy, and when Mr. Cranley had told her she had to leave, she had said firmly:

"This be my home and th' only way I'll be leaving here be in a coffin!"

Mr. Cranley had not been able to pay her.

He himself received only a very small wage from the Solicitors.

This was for acting as Caretaker at Meldon Hall.

It was the same money he had received twenty years earlier when he had first gone there.

He had hoped when the new Marquis took over that it would be increased.

What had happened was that his wages stayed the same, but now he had to pay for his food and anything else he required, which he had not had to do in the past.

He had stayed on because, as for Lucy, it had become his home and he had nowhere else to go.

Erlina had often thought it was a miserable, lonely existence.

Mr. Cranley was an educated man who had served the family to the best of his ability.

He had then been left to a life of loneliness on what was almost a starvation diet.

Still, the house was there and, as she thought about it, Erlina knew that the Vicar was right.

"It will give you a respite, Erlina," he said now, "to write to your relatives and tell them what has happened. I feel sure one of them will be able to take you in."

"I very much doubt it," Erlina answered. "As you know, Papa's brothers and sisters are all dead. The few cousins that are left live in Yorkshire, and I think there are two still alive in Cornwall."

The Vicar knew without her saying any more that she and Gerry certainly could not afford to travel such long distances.

"The first thing you have to do is to have somewhere to sleep," he said in a practical voice, "and after that we must think about your future."

"You are so kind," Erlina said.

She had noticed while they were talking that Mrs. Garnet had no egg for breakfast.

She was eating only toast with a scraping of butter.

She knew that she and Gerry must not impose on their hospitality.

Yet she had never imagined for one moment that she might live at Meldon Hall, which was an enormous house.

It had been re-built in the last century and was very impressive to look at.

Yet Erlina had heard that the whole top floor of the house was now uninhabitable.

In several of the State Bedrooms, the ceilings had fallen through because the wood had rotted from being damp.

At the same time, the structure of the building was strong.

It would take very much longer to destroy it than the cottages, which had collapsed within five years or less without attention.

The Inn, once it was closed, had quickly begun to fall into decay.

Aloud she said:

"You are quite right, Vicar. Gerry and I will go up to the Hall and ask Mr. Cranley to take us in. At least we will have plenty of room in which to move about."

She tried to speak bravely and with a smile.

But the tears were very near to the surface as she thought she would never again be able to go home.

She drank a little coffee. Then she said:

"I suppose I had better take the Daweses with me as well."

"There is nowhere for them to stay in the

village," the Vicar said, "and they might be useful in cleaning up the Hall."

"Mrs. Dawes is a good Cook when she has any ingredients," Erlina answered, "so perhaps Mr. Cranley would be pleased to have her there."

She was hoping that would be the case.

If Mr. Cranley refused to let them stay in the house, they would have to sleep in the stables with the horses.

There was, she told herself, literally no other place for them to go.

Mrs. Garnet started to clear away the plates.

The children had not left a crumb.

When Erlina looked at them, she felt that, attractive though they were, all three were too thin.

The Vicar, too, looked older than his age.

She felt her hatred for the Marquis well up inside her.

She wanted to denounce him as she had often done before.

Then she asked herself, what was the point?

He was impervious to anything that might be said of him.

It was, therefore, only poetic justice that she and Gerry should take shelter under his roof when they had nowhere else to go.

As the Vicar rose she said:

"We will go up to the Hall now, and thank you a million times for being so kind to us."

The Vicar put his hand on her shoulder.

"I wish I could do more," he said, "but you know how difficult things are."

"Of course I know," Erlina answered, "and I

only hope that wicked, wicked Marquis burns in a special Hell which is kept for people as bad as he is!"

The Vicar's eyes twinkled.

Then, as he kissed Erlina's cheek, he said:

"You know quite well that I cannot say 'Amen' to that!"

They both laughed, and somehow it broke the tension.

"I think it is spiffing that we are going to the Hall," Gerry said. "I have always wanted to explore those big rooms, but you would not let me."

"You will have your chance now," Erlina said, "and goodness knows what we may find."

"I expect it is full of ghosts!" Gerry said. "If Tom comes to see me to-morrow, we will play 'Hide and Seek.'"

Tom Garnet was about the same age as Gerry, and looked pleased at the idea.

"I would like that," he said. "May I go, Papa?"

"I see no reason why not," the Vicar replied.

Then he turned to Erlina.

"You had better not give Mr. Cranley too much of a shock," he said, "so I will send Tom up to play with Gerry as soon as you are settled in."

"I want to go, too," said Stephen, who was little more than one year younger.

"And me! And me!" cried Helen, who was only five.

"We shall all go later," the Vicar promised, "but you must understand that we cannot go to-day."

The children looked disappointed, but they were very obedient.

"I cannot come to see you this afternoon," the Vicar said to Erlina, "because I have promised my wife I will take her to the shop in the next village."

He paused a moment, and then continued:

"But I will come to-morrow, and then perhaps we can make arrangements as to how Gerry is to continue with his lessons."

Erlina had been teaching her brother in the best way she could.

It was the Vicar, however, who had taught him Latin and Arithmetic, besides giving him an interest in Literature.

It had been an excellent arrangement.

Erlina, however, was always uncomfortably conscious that they should be paying for his tuition.

As that was impossible, she could only express how grateful she was over and over again.

"I know Gerry will have no difficulty in getting into Eton," she had said only last week.

She had been wondering how she would ever find enough money to pay for the fees.

She just hoped that by some miracle something would happen before next September when he was due to take his Entrance Tests.

She had thought that the only possibility was to ignore the fact that the best pictures in the house were entailed onto Gerry's son, when he had one.

The Trustees, who were supposed to see that they were not sold, had not called at Sherwood House for over three years.

They were getting old, and it was a long journey for each of them.

"It may be cheating," Erlina said to herself, "but what is the point of having a nice picture on the wall, if Gerry is unable to go to Eton?"

She, therefore, renewed her efforts to teach him herself.

She had also been more grateful than ever to the Vicar for doing the same.

Now she could not help feeling that the large Library which she knew Meldon Hall contained would be of tremendous help to Gerry, if to nobody else.

She had never been in the Hall.

Her Father had never been particularly friendly with the last Marquis.

He, of course, met him occasionally on committees.

But the Marchioness had thought she was too grand to bother with people in the County.

With, of course, the exception of the Lord Lieutenant.

She had, therefore, not included Sir Richard and Lady Sherwood in her parties.

She had, in fact, spent more time in Meldon House in London than she did at the Hall.

It was only the Marquis who, during the last years of his life, had stayed in the country and refused to leave it.

Erlina could remember seeing the present Marquis when he was a youth, riding through the village.

She had never met him and he was eight years older than she was.

This meant that, as she was now nineteen, he was twenty-seven.

He was, she thought bitterly, old enough to know how to behave.

* * *

Climbing into the pony-cart, Erlina and Gerry waved good-bye to the Garnets.

As Erlina drove up the mile-long drive which led to Meldon Hall, she could not suppress a little thrill of excitement.

She had seen the building from a distance, but only because she had taken the liberty of riding a little way up the drive.

As she peeped at the magnificent house, it had seemed to her a mystery building simply because she had never been inside it.

Her Father and Mother had not been in the least perturbed at not being accepted by the Meldons.

Lady Sherwood had had a very sweet, gentle disposition.

She never said an unkind word about anybody.

She was also somewhat shy and reserved.

She had no desire to push herself onto people who she thought were more at home in London Society than in the country.

She was, however, an excellent rider, just as she had taught her children to be.

She was happiest when she was riding with her husband over their own land.

In the Winter they hunted with a small pack nearby, which was certainly not smart enough for the Meldons.

When her Mother was alive Erlina had felt

that the house was always filled with laughter and love.

Sometimes they had friends to stay; sometimes they were alone.

But there had always seemed to be enough to do and life was very enjoyable.

She had been sixteen when her Mother had died, and her Father fell ill shortly afterwards.

It was then that the days had seemed long and the evenings lonely.

When she and Gerry were finally alone, it was very frightening.

By this time the village was dying too, and she felt sometimes as if a great black cloud had descended over them.

It seemed to be coming closer and closer until she felt that she herself would be swallowed up.

The cause of it, of course, was the behaviour of the wicked Marquis.

It was he who had put an evil spell on everyone, from which they could not escape.

chapter two

ERLINA pulled *Nobby* up at the bottom of the long flight of steps which led to the front door.

To her surprise, she saw that the door was open.

"I tell you what we will do," she said to Gerry. "You drive *Nobby* into the stable-yard, and Dawes and Mrs. Dawes can go into the house through the Kitchen entrance. I expect the door will be open."

Gerry nodded as she went on:

"I will go in and find Mr. Cranley. Then I will come and help you unharness *Nobby*."

"All right," Gerry said.

He enjoyed driving the old pony.

As soon as Erlina got out of the pony-cart, he drove slowly towards the stables.

Erlina ran up the steps, thinking that this was the crucial moment.

If she could not persuade Mr. Cranley to let them all stay in the house, where would they go?

She walked into the hall and was aware that the stairs were thick with dust.

So was the mantelpiece on which stood a number of very fine china ornaments.

She wondered where Mr. Cranley would be.

In the old days she suspected he would have had an office where he would pay the wages and the bills, the walls covered with maps of the Estate.

There would certainly be no point in his sitting in it now.

She walked back into the hall and looked into the room on the right. The shutters were closed and it was in darkness.

She went across the all to the other side.

She saw as she walked through the door that on one of the windows the shutter had been loosened.

The deep Georgian glass window had been opened.

The rest of the room was in darkness, and she called out:

"Are you there, Mr. Cranley?"

There was no answer, and she was about to turn away and look elsewhere, when a man's voice said:

"He has gone to the village."

Erlina started, wondering who it could be.

"How annoying!" she said, "I must have just missed him. I expect he went across the Park, as I came up the drive."

There was no reply.

She thought the man must be at the other end of the room, and she went on as if she were speaking to herself:

"Anyway, if he goes to the Vicarage, the Vicar will tell him where I am, and about the ghastly . . . terrible thing . . . that has . . . happened to me."

Even as she spoke, the horror of the fire seemed to sweep over her again.

Then the man who had spoken before asked:

"What has happened to have upset you so much?"

"Anyone would . . . be upset," Erlina replied, "if the house in which they . . . lived had been . . . burnt to the . . . ground!"

"That must have been a dreadful shock!" the man agreed.

"It was ghastly, frightening, and . . . now I must . . . speak to Mr. Cranley."

"Why?"

Because she could not see the man, she did not feel he was being inquisitive.

She answered him as if it were somebody she knew and who would understand.

"My brother and I, and the old servants who . . . live with us, have simply nowhere else to . . . go."

"Surely there must be a cottage in the village in which you could stay?" the man suggested.

"In the village?" Erlina echoed. "You must be a . . . stranger in . . . these parts and Mr. Cranley cannot have . . . told you that the . . . village . . . is dead!"

She paused for a moment and then continued.

"It has died because the ... wicked ... cruel ... evil ... Marquis murdered it ... and ... all the ... people who ... lived there!"

She spoke violently.

Her feelings about what had happened seemed even more intense than they had when she had woken up that morning.

It was as if the numbness which had swept over her as she watched the fire burning everything she possessed had now evaporated.

Instead, she was feeling the horror of what had happened much more intensely than before.

"I cannot quite understand what you are saying," the stranger remarked.

"It is ... quite simple," Erlina said. "The Marquis, who, as I expect you know, owns this house, sacked all the ... people who worked on the Estate."

She continued more slowly:

"They had to go away to ... seek work ... elsewhere. The old people received no ... pensions and ... died from ... lack of food and the ... cold and rain ... which sank into their ... cottages because they were ... never repaired."

"I do not believe what I am hearing is true!" the stranger exclaimed.

"Unfortunately it is the truth," Erlina said. "My Father did what he could, but then ... the men who ... worked for us ... left too."

"Why did they do that?"

"Because there were no longer any shops in the village where they could buy food ... and even ... the Inn closed so that there was ...

nowhere for them to go for their . . . ale and cider. So when there was . . . no one left to . . . work on our land, we also . . . found it . . . hard to stay . . . alive."

She gave a deep sigh.

"Your Father, if he owned an Estate, must have had money," the stranger argued.

Again Erlina, deep in her thoughts, did not really feel that she was talking to a living person.

He was anonymous in the dark.

It was, therefore, almost as if she were answering the questions which came into her own mind.

"We had money . . . during the war," she said, "when of course . . . our crops fetched . . . good prices in the market."

She hesitated for a moment and then continued:

"But I expect you know that when peace was restored, the Farmers had to compete with cheap food coming into the country from the Continent. Many of the country Banks closed their doors. Ours was . . . one of . . . them."

She gave a little sob before she went on:

"Then my Father . . . died. He had been very . . . generous with what he could afford . . . but there was hardly enough . . . left to keep Gerry and me from . . . starving."

She tripped on the last word, then said:

"That is what is . . . happening now to . . . the Vicar. That wicked, wicked Marquis has not paid his . . . stipend, and his children are . . . thin and hungry. All he has to . . . rely on is what the Bishop gives . . . him out of . . . charity."

As she spoke the last words, she found that

27

tears were running down her cheeks.

She walked to the window so as to hide them from the man, whoever he might be, who was talking to her.

She had not cried last night when Dawes had burnt down the house.

Now the tears could not be controlled, although she did her best to wipe them away.

There was a long silence while the man in the shadows did not speak.

Then at last he said:

"Can you really be attributing all this misery to one man?"

Erlina wiped her eyes with her handkerchief and the knuckles of her left hand.

"He is . . . responsible for . . . everything!" she declared. "I was . . . saying this morning that I hope he suffers in a special . . . Hell as . . . we have all suffered, and I was . . . thinking how . . . stupid it was of my Father to have . . . saved his life when . . . he was a boy."

There was no reply from the stranger.

As if she felt she should justify the accusation, she went on:

"He was riding across a stream which had swollen in the winter rains, when his pony stumbled and threw him. He was swept away and would have . . . drowned if my Father had not plunged from his horse into the water and saved him."

"And who was your Father?" the stranger asked.

"His name was . . . Sir Richard Sherwood," Erlina answered, "and if he had let the wicked

Marquis drown, a great number of . . . villagers would still be . . . alive to-day."

Again there was silence before the man in the shadows said:

"If I remember rightly, the Sherwood Estate marches with this one, and I have often wondered who it was who saved me."

For a moment Erlina did not understand what he had said.

Then she stiffened and very slowly turned round.

"Are you . . . saying," she asked, "that—"

Even as she spoke there was the sound of footsteps outside and Gerry came to the door, shouting:

"Erlina! Erlina! Where are you?"

"I . . . I am . . . here," Erlina managed to reply.

Gerry came into the room.

"What do you think?" he asked. "There are some spiffing horses in the stables and the grooms told me that they belong to the Marquis! Do you think he is here?"

Erlina looked towards the darker part of the room.

She could vaguely see there was someone sitting in one of the armchairs in front of the fireplace.

"Wh-who are . . . you . . . ? Is it possible . . ." she stammered, "can it be . . . true that you are . . . ?"

" . . . the wicked Marquis!" the stranger finished.

"I . . . I do not . . . know what . . . to say," Erlina murmured. "How could I have . . . known that you would . . . return here without anyone . . . knowing that . . . you were . . . coming?"

"I came because it suited me to do so," the Marquis answered. "But I had no idea that my absence had caused so much chaos, if what you have been telling me is true!"

"Of course it is true," Erlina said, "and I have often . . . thought how much I would like to . . . tell you what a . . . terrible state everything is in . . . but you never . . . answered the letters which the Vicar . . . wrote to you . . . nor . . . I imagine . . . those from . . . Mr. Cranley."

"I realise now that was a mistake," the Marquis remarked slowly, "but I wished to forget this house and everything that went with it."

"But . . . how could you have been . . . so cruel? How . . . could you have . . . let all those . . . old people die?"

"That is something I did not intend," the Marquis answered. "In fact, I was not thinking of the village or of the people who lived there, but just of the house itself."

"How could you not . . . understand that the . . . people were brought up to . . . believe that . . . Meldon Hall was everything that mattered in . . . their lives? In fact they had . . . no life apart from . . . it!"

There was silence. Then Gerry said in a whisper:

"Is that really the Marquis sitting there?"

"Yes, it is," the Marquis answered.

"You have some ripping horses!" Gerry said admiringly. "If I could ride horses like those, I would never want to do anything else!"

Erlina was trying to pierce the darkness to see what the Marquis looked like.

Then in a very small voice she said:

"I . . . I suppose . . . you want us to . . . go away . . . but we . . . have . . . nowhere to . . . go."

"You said we were going to stay here," Gerry protested. "But if not, where can we go unless we sleep in the stables at home."

"That . . . is the . . . truth," Erlina said.

She walked again across the room.

"Please, Your Lordship, let us stay here for a . . . few days until we can think of . . . somewhere else where . . . we can go."

"I cannot imagine why anyone should want to stay here as it is," the Marquis said. "However, I hope to have some servants soon."

"Servants?" Erlina repeated. "But there are none available in the village."

Then she gave a little cry.

"Oh, but perhaps you will let the Daweses help you. We have brought them with us. Mrs. Dawes is a very good Cook, and Dawes knows his duties and will, I am sure, look . . . better when he is . . . having more to . . . eat."

"I suppose I am responsible for that too!" the Marquis said.

"You will not . . . like my . . . saying so . . . but it is the . . . truth," Erlina answered.

To her surprise, there came a laugh from the other side of the room.

"I may as well be hanged for a sheep as a lamb!" the Marquis said. "But I will certainly take the Daweses in, and anybody else who can provide for me."

There was silence. Then Erlina said hesitatingly:

"As Gerry and . . . I have . . . nothing left . . . except for the . . . clothes we stand up in . . . and there are only a few . . . pounds left in the . . . Bank . . . we will . . . work for you . . . if you will have us."

"And what do you suggest you could do for me?" the Marquis enquired.

Erlina made a little gesture with her hands.

"Anything you . . . require. I can be your . . . Housekeeper until you find . . . someone more experienced . . . which might be difficult in this . . . part of . . . the world. Or I could . . . clean your house as I have been . . . cleaning our own since . . . my Father died."

"Very well, Miss Sherwood," the Marquis agreed. "You can run the house for me, and help Cranley engage what servants he can find."

"You are not . . . thinking of bringing . . . any from London?" Erlina asked.

"No!"

The monosyllable was sharp. Erlina realised that the suggestion had annoyed him.

Gerry, who had been listening to the conversation, said:

"I do not know what I can do, unless I help look after the horses."

"How old are you?" the Marquis asked.

"I am eleven and three months," Gerry replied. "But I am very strong."

"Then I certainly think you should help with the horses and exercise them," the Marquis said.

"Do you mean—ride them?"

"If you are a good rider."

Gerry gave a whoop of joy.

"I am a very, very good rider! Tell him, Erlina, tell him I am good."

"I have always considered you are," Erlina said, "but then, we have not had very well-bred horses."

"I will be very careful with your horses," Gerry promised, "and thank you, thank you for saying I can ride them."

He turned towards the door.

"I will just go and have another look at them," he said. "The grooms are grumbling that the stables want cleaning and there are tiles off the roof."

He went from the room, and the Marquis said in an amused voice:

"I suppose that is my fault, too!"

"There have been no repairs done to the house any more than there have in the village," Erlina replied. "I have heard, although I have not seen it myself, that the roof is in a bad state and the ceilings have fallen in some of the State Rooms."

"It will be your job, Miss Sherwood," the Marquis said, "to ensure that they are repaired as quickly as possible."

"Do you . . . really mean that?" Erlina asked. "Are you seriously going . . . to let Gerry and me live here?"

"Despite the fact that you are frightened and look on me in horror," the Marquis replied, "that is what I intend."

"But why?" Erlina asked. "Why should you suddenly have changed . . . your mind after all . . . these years of not even . . . communicating with . . . anybody?"

The Marquis did not reply, and she went on:

"Mr. Cranley has had . . . a struggle to keep . . . alive on the very small wage he is being . . . paid as . . . Caretaker and after Lucy . . . died— you remember Lucy?"

She paused before she said:

"He has been . . . alone in this . . . big house and could not . . . afford even to have anyone . . . clean it, even if there had been . . . anybody left in the . . . village who would . . . do so."

The Marquis was silent.

Then Erlina thought she had been rude.

He might change his mind about letting them stay, so she said quickly:

"I had better . . . start by opening . . . the shutters. It is depressing to sit in the dark."

"You may open the shutters," the Marquis replied, "but it will make no difference to me."

Erlina had already gone to one of the other windows and, pulling back the shutter, said over her shoulder:

"Why should it make no difference?"

There was no answer.

She opened the shutters wide and the sunlight came streaming into the room.

There were two more windows to open, but already she could see clearly.

She looked across to where the Marquis was sitting by the fireplace.

As she did so, she gave a little cry.

Covering his eyes was a black bandage.

"Oh!" she exclaimed. "I did not realise . . . I had no idea . . ."

"That I am blind?" the Marquis said. "Now you will understand why I have come home."

The way he spoke made her answer perceptively:

"Because you did not wish to be seen."

"Exactly," he agreed. "The Oculist told me that I am to keep my eyes bandaged and be completely in the dark if there is to be any chance of my seeing again."

"I am sorry . . . very sorry . . . it must be . . . terrible for you."

"It is the Hell that you have been wishing me to suffer."

Erlina was silent for a moment.

Then she asked:

"How did it . . . happen? Did you have an . . . accident?"

"The bough of a tree hit me across the eyes when I was taking part in a Steeple-Chase at night."

"Was that not . . . rather dangerous?"

"It was very dangerous," he agreed. "The riders had their left arms bound to their sides, and were all blind drunk!"

"I have heard of these Steeple-Chases taking place amongst the Bucks and *Beaux,*" Erlina said, "and I always thought it a . . . very silly and . . . dangerous thing . . . to do."

"It was a challenge," the Marquis said defensively.

"You might have . . . killed yourself," Erlina murmured.

"One of the competitors in fact was killed, and another was severely injured."

"How could you be so . . . stupid? How could you . . . risk what, after all . . . is the most . . .

35

precious possession you have—your life?"

"I did not think of that at the time," the Marquis said, "but, of course, Miss Sherwood, you are quite right."

He spoke in a mocking, cynical manner.

Because it made Erlina feel embarrassed, she turned to the next window and started to release the shutters.

"It is unnecessary to go to all that trouble," the Marquis said. "All I can see is darkness, darkness, darkness! You are quite right, Miss Sherwood, it is an unmitigated Hell!"

Erlina sighed.

Now that she could see him clearly, she realised that he was an extremely handsome man.

His hair was swept back from his forehead.

Despite the black bandage, she could see he had fine features and a square, rather aggressive chin.

He was dressed in the height of fashion, with an intricately tied white cravat.

He wore a whipcord coat over a champagne-coloured waistcoat, which matched his pantaloons.

His boots shone as if, as Erlina had heard but had not believed, they had been cleaned with champagne.

She stood for a moment, looking at him.

Then she said very quietly:

"If you are to get well, which of course you want to do, you have to believe that this is only a . . . temporary affliction."

"Are you preaching at me?" the Marquis asked.

"I am trying to make you understand that good

health has not only to do with our physical bodies, but also our minds, and although you may not like the word—our souls."

"I thought you were certain I did not have one!" the Marquis argued.

"It should be a . . . challenge to prove I am . . . wrong," Erlina said quickly, and saw the smile on his lips.

"Can you really be concerned, after all you have said, with my well-being?" the Marquis asked.

Again there was that mocking note in his voice.

"As your employee, My Lord," Erlina replied, "it is my . . . duty to be concerned with your food and your well-being, and that is what I hope you will be . . . paying me . . . to do."

She thought as she spoke that perhaps she was being somewhat outrageous in what she was saying.

At the same time, the words seemed to come to her lips without her thinking what she should say.

Again the Marquis laughed.

"You are making my home-coming very different from what I expected."

Erlina walked to the last window.

"Without wishing to be in the least impertinent," she said, "I am very . . . very . . . curious as to why you have not come . . . home before."

"Do you really want to know?" the Marquis enquired.

She opened the fourth window, thinking the sunshine and the fresh air would sweep away the mustiness in the room.

Then she walked back to the fireplace.

Because she knew that he could not see her, she sat down in a chair near to his.

She suddenly felt as if the shock of what had happened made it difficult for her legs to support her.

And yet, he was so different from anything she had expected, that she wanted to go on talking to the Marquis.

He was not looking as frightening as she had expected he would.

When she had thought about him before and had positively hated him, he had seemed to her a personification of the Devil.

Now she could imagine how frustrating it must be for a man who was obviously very athletic to be completely blind.

The black bandage looked as if it was wound very tightly round his head, but she was sure the Oculist had insisted on that.

If it was at all loose, it might let in the light at the sides.

"Do you really want to know why I have done all those things for which you have condemned me?" the Marquis asked. "It was because I was so desperately unhappy here when I was your brother's age."

"Unhappy?" Erlina exclaimed.

It was something she had never imagined.

"My Mother never appeared to be very fond of me," the Marquis went on, "and my Father was a martinet. He believed that children should be treated as if they were raw recruits, to be bullied and whipped into unquestioning obedience until they had no will of their own."

"And that . . . really happened to . . . you?" Erlina asked.

"I used to cry myself to sleep every night that I was here," the Marquis answered. "The only time I could escape from what seemed to be persecution by my Father was when I was at School."

He paused for a moment before he went on:

"I dreaded the holidays. I used to feel a shrinking feeling inside me as I came up the drive, and the moment I stepped into the Hall I felt sick with apprehension about what would happen when my Father saw me."

"I was aware that my Father never liked yours," Erlina said, "and your Mother did not think we were grand enough to know. But of course I had no idea that anything like that was happening. We were always so very happy in our house."

"Mine was like a prison—a torture-chamber. It burned itself into my mind so that once I was old enough I vowed revenge on what to me had been a place of misery."

Erlina sighed.

"Now I can understand why you acted the way you did. But surely, when you received letters from the Vicar and other people that, I suppose, told you what the situation was, you had some idea of what you were allowing to happen?"

"To be truthful, I never read the letters," the Marquis said. "They were opened by my Secretary, and when he said the words 'Meldon Hall' I told him to throw them into the wastepaper-basket."

"If only we had . . . understood that was

how . . . you were . . . feeling," Erlina said in a low voice.

"Would it have made things any better?" the Marquis asked.

"I suppose . . . not," she admitted, "but everything has been so . . . ghastly this last year or so with nobody left in the village except for a few old people, who are incapable of going anywhere else."

She was thinking of Henry as she spoke.

She knew there were two other old men left in the village and an old woman who was too weak to leave her bed.

The Vicar himself had put tarpaulins over the roofs of their cottages to keep out the rain.

They had somehow managed to survive, though they were all very feeble.

"What are you going to do now?" she asked.

As if the Marquis had followed her thoughts, he said:

"You have forced me, Miss Sherwood, into accepting one challenge. I suppose, therefore, I shall have to accept another one."

"What do you mean by that?" Erlina asked.

"I dare say," he said sarcastically, "you are only too willing to tell me what I have to do. Although I cannot resurrect the dead, I can do something for those who are still living."

Erlina drew in her breath.

"Do you . . . mean that? . . . Do you . . . really mean . . . it?"

"I have no alternative," the Marquis answered. "Like all women, you will doubtless nag me into doing what you want. It will be quite easy for you because I cannot fight for myself since I am blind."

"I am quite sure, My Lord, that it would be impossible to make you do anything you did not want to do," Erlina said. "But now that you know what has been happening, I feel equally sure you will want to make the village a living place once again."

"Now you are trying the feminine approach," the Marquis said.

Erlina felt almost as if he had hit her.

She rose from the chair in which she was sitting.

The Marquis put out his hand to stay her.

"Forgive me, and do not go away," he begged, "I have been in a fiendish bad humour since I had this accident and was told I had to remain blind-folded for perhaps months until my eyes healed."

He paused for a moment and then said:

"I thought at first I would stay in London and be entertained by the amusing people I call my friends."

"Why did you not do so?" Erlina asked.

"Because I found almost at once that people never behave quite normally to a man who is blind. They say soothing, ingratiating things as if they were talking to an idiot, and many of them raised their voices as if they thought I was also deaf."

Erlina sat down again.

"Now you will understand what I was saying to you just now," she said. "To get well again you have to use your brain and your perception, and that is what is already beginning to work."

The Marquis did not speak, but he was listening as she went on:

"Because you cannot see, other parts of your anatomy are beginning to work. You are aware when people are placating you, which is something you very likely would not have noticed before, when you had your sight."

Erlina thought for a moment, then continued:

"I think, too, that when people are blind, they are more attuned to the wonder and the beauty of nature. That is why your instinct told you that you should come to the country."

"Who taught you all this?" the Marquis asked.

"My Mother, who was very interested in anything spiritual and also had a great knowledge of herbs. We had an Herb Garden which sadly is now overgrown. But I am sure I can find something that will help to strengthen your eyes and make them heal quickly if you use it every day."

She paused before she asked:

"Will you do that?"

"I suppose," the Marquis replied, "if you are going to run my house, you will also run me, and I shall have to do what you tell me."

"That is certainly a step in the right direction," Erlina said as she smiled.

Then she laughed.

"Why are you laughing?" the Marquis asked.

"Because I cannot believe this is happening," she replied. "I have hated and hated you! I prayed to God, although I tried not to, that He would punish you for what I thought was your cruelty and your wickedness."

"And He has so very efficiently!" the Marquis said sharply.

"That may have been a punishment," Erlina said. "At the same time, it has brought you home and given you a chance to redeem yourself by helping those who are still alive."

"And you are just waiting to give me a list of them!" the Marquis suggested.

"Of course!" Erlina agreed in a different tone of voice. "We can start with the Vicar, and then Mr. Cranley."

"Before I brace myself for another lecture," the Marquis said, "I would appreciate something to drink, and perhaps a good luncheon."

Erlina laughed.

"And where do you think that is to come from?"

"You will find that I have brought a case of champagne down with me in case the cellar has run dry," the Marquis said, "but I had not thought of food."

"I will go and see if there is anything available which Mrs. Dawes can cook for you," Erlina said, "and as you have brought grooms here with you, it would be sensible if we could send one to the next village to buy some provisions."

The Marquis made a gesture with his hands.

"That comes under your department, Miss Sherwood," he said.

Erlina's heart gave a little leap.

Then she said:

"Do you mean . . . that I can order . . . anything I want?"

"Of course," the Marquis agreed, "and I may tell you that I am very particular as to what I eat and expect only the best."

"Now I know I am dreaming!" Erlina cried. "I can only hope I do not wake up too quickly!"

She ran from the room while she was still speaking.

She crossed the hall towards a long corridor which she was sure would lead to the Kitchens.

As she did so, she thought she heard the Marquis laughing.

chapter three

ERLINA ran down the corridor to what she thought was the Kitchen door.

When she opened it she saw to her astonishment that there were five men, as well as Mr. and Mrs. Dawes, seated at the table.

Gerry was also there, eating a large sandwich with great joy.

For a moment the men stared at her before they rose to their feet.

She went towards them.

"I expect Dawes will already have told you," she said, "that I am Miss Sherwood. The Marquis has now asked me to run the house for him, and I need you all desperately."

They still stared, and she turned to Dawes and said:

"Dawes, His Lordship wants a glass of champagne at once, and you are now engaged as his Butler, with Mrs. Dawes as his Cook."

Mrs. Dawes flung out her arms in delight before she started to cry.

"I thinks we'd die of starvation," she sobbed. "Can what you're a-sayin' really be true?"

"It is true," Erlina said quickly, "but there is no time for you to be crying, Mrs. Dawes, because His Lordship requires his luncheon."

"An' what am I to cook, I'd like to know?" Mrs. Dawes asked.

She had stopped crying, and Erlina knew she was waiting for an answer.

"We will have to buy some food," she said, and held out her hand to the nearest man. "Please tell me who you are."

"Oi' be Jacob th' coachman," he answered, "an' this 'ere's Sam th' footman."

He indicated the man beside him.

Erlina guessed even before the other two men introduced themselves that they were Outriders.

At the end of the table was a man she was sure would be the Marquis's Valet.

She was not mistaken.

As she shook his hand he said:

"I'm Hignet, Miss, an' I was wiv 'Is Lordship when he were in th' Army."

"Then I shall look especially to you to help me," Erlina said. "We have to cure his eyes, and also keep him in a good temper until he can see again."

"That's just what I was thinkin' meself, Miss," Hignet agreed.

"Now, what about luncheon?" Erlina asked. "I

thought perhaps you, Jacob, and Sam would ride over to the next village and buy everything that Mrs. Dawes needs."

"That'll be everythin' you can think of, an' more," Mrs. Dawes piped up.

"Make a list," Erlina said, "and, as those who have come from London with him will know, His Lordship wants the best."

Mrs. Dawes gave a little cry of excitement, and opening a kitchen-drawer looked for a piece of paper on which to write.

Hignet said in a quiet voice:

"Seein' as 'ow 'Is Lordship ain't been 'ome for six years, Miss, I took th' liberty of not only bringin' th' champagne down wi' us, but also some food."

"That is the most wonderful thing I could hear!" Erlina exclaimed. "Thank you for being so clever."

She knew that Hignet was delighted with her praise.

He then explained that among other things he had brought with him a pâté, which the Chef in London had made.

There was also an uncooked leg of lamb, and a large cold ham, of which they were already eating large slices.

When she looked at Dawes she thought he appeared spry and even looked a little younger.

It was a long time since they had been able to afford meat, unless one counted the few rabbits he had been able to snare.

"Would you like a cup o' tea, Miss?" Mrs. Dawes enquired.

"I would love one!" Erlina answered.

Tea, being more expensive than the inferior

coffee they had been drinking, was something she could not afford.

She saw that everybody round the table was drinking tea, with the exception of Gerry.

He had a glass of what looked like lemonade.

He pushed the last piece of sandwich into his mouth, saying:

"That ham was jolly good, Erlina, you should have some."

"I will later," Erlina replied. "I have a great deal to do first."

She took Mrs. Dawes to one side of the Kitchen, and wrote out the long list of what she required.

She knew Mrs. Dawes could write, but only very laboriously.

The list took up both sides of two pieces of paper.

When they had finished, Erlina went back to the table, and handed the list to the coachman. Then, looking at Hignet, she said:

"You must help me. Do we ask His Lordship for money? It might be difficult to open an account so quickly."

"'Is Lordship trusts me wiv 'is money," Hignet said.

He drew from his pocket a large bank-note and handed it to Erlina.

She in turn gave it to the coachman and said:

"Please go as quickly as you can and, while you are in the next village, perhaps you could mention that we are looking for staff. We need at least two or three people in the Kitchen to help Mrs. Dawes, and Dawes will want four footmen."

Both Mr. and Mrs. Dawes stared at her as if

she were speaking in a foreign language.

Then, as she and Gerry went from the Kitchen, she heard them all talking at the tops of their voices.

As they reached the hall, Erlina saw the Vicar coming up the steps.

"I suppose Mr. Cranley has been to see you," she said.

"He has," the Vicar replied, "and I can hardly believe that after all these years, His Lordship has returned home."

"He is waiting to see you," Erlina said.

Then she dropped her voice as she went on:

"I do not know if Mr. Cranley told you, but he is temporarily blind."

"Cranley did say that he has suffered an injury to his eyes," the Vicar replied.

"They are closely bandaged and he can see nothing," Erlina said. "I think you will be surprised at what he has to tell you."

"I have already heard," the Vicar told her.

Erlina walked ahead of him into the Sitting-Room.

"The Vicar is here, My Lord," she said, "and I know he will be a great help in what is to be a colossal undertaking."

The Vicar walked across the room.

"I am delighted to see you home again, My Lord," he said. "It is a very long time since we have seen each other, but I expect you remember me?"

"Of course I do," the Marquis answered. "And you have surely been laying a curse on me in the same way that Miss Sherwood has."

49

"As a Clergyman, I tried not to, but instead sought some explanation for Your Lordship's absence."

"I doubt if you were successful," the Marquis replied dryly. "Now that I am back, I need your help."

"You know I am only too willing to give it," the Vicar promised.

"Miss Sherwood has already told me that, like everybody else, you have been badly treated," the Marquis said. "I must, therefore, Vicar, put that right before we start on anybody else."

The Vicar did not speak, and the Marquis asked:

"What stipend were you receiving when my Father was alive?"

"Three-hundred pounds a year, My Lord," the Vicar replied, "but of course it ceased on your Father's death."

"Then why, considering you were not paid, did you not leave Meldon?" the Marquis asked.

"The people I had looked after for a number of years needed me," the Vicar said simply. "Even when they were dying from cold and starvation they wanted me to be there, and I could not abandon them."

Erlina, listening, knew that the Marquis could not fail to notice his sincerity.

There was silence until the Marquis said:

"I am very grateful to you, which is something I never expected to say in Meldon. In future, you will receive five-hundred pounds a year, and as soon as Cranley returns, he will make you out a Note of Hand for what you are owed for the five years since my father's death. That will amount to twenty-five-hundred pounds."

For a moment the Vicar could not speak.

Then he said in a somewhat unsteady voice:

"Did—did you say—twenty-five-hundred pounds—My Lord?"

"I think that would be fair and, as soon as you find me the largest and most reliable Firm to repair the cottages in the village, we shall start on the Vicarage."

"I think I am dreaming!" the Vicar murmured.

Erlina laughed.

"That is what I have been thinking ever since I found His Lordship here."

"Things are already being put in their right place," the Marquis said sharply, "but we have to face reality. Cranley has doubtless told you that I sent him to find servants to staff the house. Is it possible to persuade people to come back to the village or for new people to settle here?"

"I have kept in touch with some of those who have left," the Vicar said, "and I think a fair number of them would be happy to return to Meldon if the village is restored to what it was when they lived here. Others, however, may be too bitter to do so."

"Then the first thing is to make the place habitable," the Marquis said, "and to see that my own roof does not collapse on my head."

The Vicar looked at Erlina.

"It will be a big job," he said.

"However big, I want it done immediately," the Marquis insisted. "I may be blind, but I have no wish to be uncomfortable as well!"

"I am sure Erlina will do everything in her power to prevent you from suffering any more than can be avoided," the Vicar said quietly, "and if you can put back the clock, then I am sure a great number of people, including myself, will bless you for doing so."

"That is better than bearing the burden of your curses!" the Marquis said a little cynically. "Which I am sure Miss Sherwood thinks is a direct punishment from Heaven for the manner in which I have behaved."

"If we are going to turn over a new leaf and get you well," Erlina said, "you will have to forget the past and think only of the future."

The Vicar smiled at her.

"You are quite right," he said, "but His Lordship must understand it will be a Herculean task not only to re-build the village, but also to restore the land which has been allowed to run wild for these past five years."

"I want competent men who know their job," the Marquis said, "and they will work not only on Meldon soil, but also on Miss Sherwood's Estate, next to mine."

"That is not as important as yours," Erlina said quickly.

"Not so, they are equally important." The Marquis contradicted her. "And it is part of the price I am prepared to pay for your services."

Erlina gave a little laugh, and said to the Vicar:

"When I came to you in despair last night, I never imagined that today I would not only have somewhere to live with Gerry, but also have a very difficult but fascinating job. His Lordship,

52

as you realise, is employing me and Mr. and Mrs. Dawes, who are ecstatic at knowing they can have a square meal again."

Even as she spoke, Dawes came in carrying a silver tray that wanted cleaning.

On it was a bottle of champagne and a number of glasses.

He had, Erlina noticed, brushed his hair and straightened his neck-tie.

In fact, he looked quite respectable as he came across the room and set down the tray on a small table by the fireplace.

"Shall I pour out th' champagne, M'Lord?" he asked in a respectful voice.

"Yes, of course," the Marquis answered, "and I am delighted that you and your wife are here to work for me."

"We're very, very grateful to Your Lordship for having us," Dawes replied.

He poured out the champagne.

He handed first a glass to Erlina, then one to the Marquis, and one to the Vicar.

"Can I have some champagne?" Gerry asked. "I have never tasted it."

"You can have a sip of mine," Erlina answered.

She handed him her glass, and Gerry took a cautious sip.

"It is not bad," he said, "but I think I like lemonade better."

"That is very sensible of you," the Marquis said. "You stick to lemonade until you are my age."

"I have been to see your horses again," Gerry answered, "and they are more comfortable than they were when they first arrived. But now two of them have to go shopping."

The Marquis smiled.

"That will be a new experience for them, and to-morrow, if they are not too tired, you must ride whichever one you fancy."

"Thank you, thank you!" Gerry cried. "I will just go to see which ones they are taking shopping."

He ran from the room, and Erlina said:

"There is no doubt as to who will be the happiest person in Meldon now that you have returned. Gerry has always been obsessed with horses, like our Father. But we had only three rather old ones. I was wondering, My Lord, if you would allow me to bring the two that are left at Sherwood House into your stables?"

"Of course you must bring them here," the Marquis replied. "Send my Outriders over immediately to fetch them. They can lead them back."

"I think what I will do, if you will allow me," Erlina said, "is to send Gerry with them to show them the way, and he can ride one of the horses back."

"That is a good idea," the Vicar said. "Gerry is a very good rider, and Your Lordship can trust him."

"I am trusting both you and Miss Sherwood to carry out my instructions," the Marquis said, "and that is to get busy right away. I want everything done as quickly as possible."

"We can but try," the Vicar said. "I have never been given a task which is nearer to my heart, and I am exceedingly grateful for it, both to Your Lordship and, of course, to God."

"If you and Miss Sherwood preach at me much longer," the Marquis said, "I shall really believe it is God who has visited my blindness upon me, not only to punish me for my sins, but also to make quite certain that I make reparation for them."

"That appears to me to be a reasonable view," the Vicar said.

He spoke with a note of amusement in his voice.

Just for a moment Erlina held her breath, in case the Marquis thought it was insulting.

Instead of which he laughed.

"I have always been suspicious," he said, "of people who twist the Bible to make it say what they want it to say."

"I think that is forgivable if they need it very badly," the Vicar replied.

Because Dawes had left the room, Erlina refilled the Marquis's glass from the bottle of champagne, then the Vicar's.

"If you will look after His Lordship," she said to the Vicar, "I am going upstairs to see what the condition is of the rooms on the First Floor."

"By all means do so," the Vicar replied. "I hope that at least some of them are undamaged, but of course the beds will need airing."

"That is what I was thinking," Erlina answered.

She went from the room as the Vicar sat down beside the Marquis.

Outside in the hall she found Hignet.

"I am just going up to look at the bedrooms," she told him. "Will you come with me to see if His Lordship's, at any rate, is habitable?"

"That's just what I were about to do, Miss," Hignet replied. "This be a fine 'ouse if it wasn't for the dust and dirt of ages."

"Mr. Cranley has done his best to keep it habitable," Erlina said, "but, as you can imagine, for one man by himself it was a hopeless task."

They walked up what was a magnificent staircase to the First Floor.

The State Rooms opened off a wide corridor.

The first two or three they looked at seemed livable, if very dusty with cobwebs everywhere.

In another some birds had somehow crept in and built nests on the cornices below the ceilings.

In two other rooms the ceilings had fallen down, making a mess over what Erlina knew was an Aubusson carpet.

To her delight, however, the Master Suite was in good condition.

It was, of course, thick with dust and the fireplace had not been cleared of ashes since it was last used.

But the huge four-poster bed, with its carved posts and gilded canopy, had not been affected by the passing years.

The red velvet curtains needed shaking, but the Marquis's Coat-of-Arms embroidered above the headboard was undamaged.

"We need hot bedpans to air the mattresses," Erlina said. "I am sure there must be plenty of them somewhere in the house."

She was not to be disappointed.

There were a number of them hanging on the wall of the housemaids' cupboard.

She saw with delight that the Linen Cupboard, which still smelled of lavender, was filled with clean sheets and pillow-cases.

"It says a great deal for the people in the village," Erlina said, "that none of these things have been stolen while the house has been empty with only one man to guard it."

"I were just thinkin' that," Hignet agreed, "but from what I 'ears from Mr. Dawes, they be too weak to walk up the drive, an' too 'ungry to want anythin' but food."

"That is true," Erlina said in a low voice, "and I am afraid that however much His Lordship tries to put things right, these last few years will never be forgotten."

"Now, don't you go thinkin' like that, Miss," Hignet said. "We was often 'ungry, cold, and miserable in Portugal, but when 'twere all over an' we'd won th' Battle of Waterloo, we'd all but forgotten th' bad times and thinks only o' th' good."

"I hope you are right," Erlina said, "and one day I hope you will tell me about the Battle of Waterloo."

" 'Is Lordship were brave as a lion!" Hignet said, "an' when the Duke o' Wellin'ton give 'im a medal for gallantry, 'e says no-one deserved it more than 'e did!"

Erlina thought that this was something she had never expected to hear about the Marquis.

Yet, even if she had, it was doubtful if she would have thought any better of him.

They went through a number of other rooms, and Erlina decided it was best for her and Gerry to be on this floor until the roof was repaired.

She also insisted that the coachman, footman, and the Outriders, with, of course, Hignet, should be on the First Floor of the South Wing.

"It would be a great mistake," she explained, "for anyone to go higher until the roof is properly repaired. I saw how quickly our own roof collapsed in the fire. I do not want to take the risk of anyone sleeping under this one until we know it is safe."

"That be kind o' ye, Miss, an' I agrees wi' every word ye say," Hignet replied.

It took them some time, because the house was so big, to inspect just the First Floor in the centre block.

When she went downstairs again, Erlina found that the Vicar had gone home and the Marquis was alone.

She told him what they had been doing, and he listened attentively.

Then she added a little nervously:

"You must tell me exactly what . . . you want . . . to do. The first thing is whether you wish to have luncheon in the Dining-Room, and I assume you would prefer to be alone."

The Marquis was silent for a moment. Then he said:

"Yesterday I should certainly have said 'alone,' as I did not want anybody to see me making a fool of myself while eating. But today we have so much to discuss and I have so much to hear about my possessions, that you and Gerry will eat with me."

"You are . . . quite sure . . . that you . . . want us?" Erlina asked.

"I want you," the Marquis confirmed, "and as you are looking after me, you can cut up my food, which Hignet has been doing for me."

"I shall like being with you," Erlina said without thinking.

"That is certainly an admission in the right direction!" the Marquis said mockingly.

"You were very kind to the Vicar," Erlina went on, "and I am very grateful."

"Did that matter so much to you?" the Marquis enquired unexpectedly.

"Of course it did," she replied. "He is a part of my life just as the people in the village were part of my life from the time I was a child."

She paused for a moment before she added:

"Perhaps you do not understand because you have been in the war, and have travelled, and have lived in London. But I have lived only here. Unless you invite people to stay and talk to you, I am afraid you are going to find my conversation very dull."

There was silence before the Marquis said:

"I am using my perception, as you told me to do, and although you may have lived only in one place physically, I think you have travelled in many parts of the world in your mind."

Erlina clapped her hands.

"That is very clever of you, and exactly true. I am sure, also, that when you were talking to the Vicar you realised what a good, sincere man he is."

"I thought while you were listening that that was what you thought I should be thinking," the Marquis said.

Erlina laughed.

"You are the best pupil I have ever had," she said. "If you go on like this, I shall soon be learning from you rather than you learning from me."

"Perhaps we have a great deal to teach each other," the Marquis said.

There was a little pause before he added:

"I think you and I should make a pact, Erlina— I am bored with calling you 'Miss Sherwood'—to be honest with each other."

"But of course!" Erlina agreed.

"You have been honest in telling me how much you hated me, and I have confessed to you the reason for my behaviour," the Marquis went on. "I have a feeling, although I may be wrong, that there will be a great many problems in the future which we will have to share if we are to put things right."

He paused a moment, and then went on:

"I want you to stop being afraid of me, and always tell me the truth."

"I promise, I promise," Erlina answered, "and talking to you will be exactly like talking to Papa . . . before he fell ill. He was so clever and had seen so much of the world that he made me see it through his eyes."

She paused, then said a little shyly:

"I am thinking that . . . perhaps for . . . the moment . . . you could . . . use my . . . eyes."

"That is what I want to do," the Marquis answered, "but you do promise you will always tell me the truth?"

He put out his hand as he spoke, and Erlina put her hand into it.

"I promise," she said softly.

* * *

Luncheon was late, but when it came, Erlina, who by this time was very hungry, thought it was the most delicious meal she had ever eaten.

They sat in the beautiful Dining-Room designed by Robert Adam.

It had alcoves in which stood statues of Gods and Goddesses of Greece.

The walls were painted in the green that was the Adams' particular colour.

The ceiling was an exceptionally fine one.

The marble fireplace wanted cleaning, so did the windows and the sideboards.

But Dawes had managed to get the dust off the polished table.

Erlina thought that with a few more cleanings it would look as it had at the beginning of the century, when the Prince of Wales, as he then was, had made it fashionable not to use a table cloth.

The Marquis sat at the top of the table, with Erlina on his right and Gerry on his left.

Dawes, looking more like himself than he had for years, handed round the dishes which were brought from the Kitchen.

They were placed on the sideboard by Hignet and one of the Outriders.

They started with the pâté which Hignet had brought down from London.

Then came the leg of lamb which had been excellently roasted by Mrs. Dawes.

Somebody must have found some vegetables in the kitchen-garden which was close to the stables.

There were even a few very small potatoes which might have been dug up quickly.

Because he knew they were hungry, Dawes gave

Erlina and Gerry very large helpings.

She doubted if she would get through it all.

She cut up some thin slices of lamb for the Marquis.

He managed to eat it very elegantly, she noticed, without dropping anything on the table or down his clothes.

She was certain he was very fastidious.

She could understand the reason why at first he wanted to eat by himself and not have anybody watching him.

To make the Marquis feel at ease, she talked, but not about the village or the sufferings of the people.

Instead, she discussed the places in the world her Father had visited.

Then she told him of her Mother's interest in herbs which promoted healing.

"I think some people thought Mama was a White Witch," she said, "but they all came to her. And as the only Doctor in the vicinity was several miles away, no-one sent for him unless they were dying or had broken an arm or a leg."

"And you have carried on where your Mother left off," the Marquis suggested.

"I am not nearly as knowledgeable as Mama was," Erlina replied, "but I try to remember exactly what she told me. While Gerry and I were trying to keep the house clean, we used also to do some weeding in the Herb Garden."

She could not help thinking that this sort of conversation must bore the Marquis.

He was used to the wit and chatter of the smartest people in London Society.

Hignet brought in the last course.

It was cheese which he had brought down from London.

When he had left the room, Erlina said to the Marquis:

"Now it is your turn to tell me about the places you have been to and the things you have done. And both Gerry and I are longing to hear about the Battle of Waterloo, and the medal you won."

"I suppose Hignet has been talking to you!" the Marquis said. "He makes so much fuss about that medal that he might have won it himself!"

"I am sure he deserved one," Erlina said, "and he has been so helpful already that I am prepared to award him a dozen medals, if he goes on the way he has started."

"I want to hear about the Battle of Waterloo," Gerry insisted.

He had not said very much during the meal.

Now, after he had drunk a little of his lemonade, he wiped his mouth and looked expectantly at the Marquis.

For a moment Erlina thought he would refuse to discuss the battle.

Then, as if he did not wish to disappoint Gerry, he started to tell him what he wanted to know.

How the Prussian Guards had come to the rescue of the British Forces who were outnumbered.

How, almost at the last minute, the tide had turned and Napoleon had been defeated.

Gerry listened wide-eyed, and the Marquis finished by saying:

"When I am able to see again, I will draw you a

map so that you can see how the Regiments were lined up against each other."

"I would like that," Gerry replied excitedly.

"But make no mistake, Gerry," the Marquis went on, "war is wrong, cruel, and very unpleasant. There are moments of elation when a Battle has been won, but victory demands a terrible price in human suffering and loss of life."

"I did not think about that," Gerry replied.

"Then think about it now," the Marquis answered, "and while you love horses, you must be aware that hundreds of horses died, or were wounded in battle. Their screams when they were hit by a cannon-ball is something I can never forget!"

He spoke very earnestly.

Again Erlina thought he was very different from what she had expected of the man she had hated and had prayed would suffer.

Unexpectedly she found herself saying a different prayer.

She thought that if it surprised her, it would, if he were aware of it, certainly surprise the Marquis.

"Please, God," she was saying in her heart, "let him be able to . . . see again."

chapter four

ERLINA burst into the Drawing-Room, where the Marquis was sitting, and exclaimed:

"I have found it! I have found it!"

"What have you found?" the Marquis asked.

"The Fennel and the Eyebright for your eyes."

"In your Herb Garden, I suppose," the Marquis said.

"Yes, and it was easy to find the Fennel, but very difficult to find the Eyebright, because it is so small."

"I do not suppose they will do any good," the Marquis said rather ungratefully.

Erline drew in her breath.

"You are not very encouraging," she said, "and it took me a long time to . . . find them."

The way she spoke sounded tragic.

Unexpectedly the Marquis held out his hand.

"Come here," he said.

Reluctantly she moved a little closer to him, then, as his hand was still outstretched, put hers into it.

"I think," the Marquis said quietly, "it upset you going back and seeing your house."

Erlina's fingers tightened on his.

Then she answered in a broken little voice:

"It . . . was terrible . . . awful! There are just . . . a few bits of the walls . . . standing, and ashes which . . . are still . . . smouldering."

As if she could not bear the thought, she sank down on her knees beside the Marquis, taking her hand away from his.

"What will . . . become of . . . Gerry and . . . me?" she asked. "What . . . shall we . . . do? Where . . . can we . . . go?"

There was a frantic note in her voice.

"I thought you were happy here," the Marquis said.

"We are . . . of course . . . we are!" Erlina said. "But we . . . cannot stay for . . . ever. Sometime . . . you will get . . . married and . . . then . . ."

"I shall never marry!" the Marquis remarked sharply.

The way he spoke was so surprising that Erlina looked up at him, her eyes wide in her pale face.

"Never . . . marry?" she repeated. "But . . . why not?"

There was a pause as if the Marquis was reluctant to answer the question.

Then he said:

"One cannot trust a beautiful woman not to

behave as my Mother did, not interested in her husband or, for that matter, in me."

Erlina sat back on her heels.

"You may have thought like that in the . . . past," she said, "but now you are . . . different. You have learnt not to look with your eyes . . . but with your . . . heart."

The Marquis did not answer, but she knew he was listening and she went on:

"How do you think you . . . knew just now that I was . . . upset at seeing my home? You could not see me, and I was . . . determined as I came back that you should . . . not know I had been . . . upset."

"All right," the Marquis said, "I agree that I do use my instinct more than I used to when I could look at people and believe what they told me without realising it was all lies."

"That is at . . . least an advance," Erlina answered, "and I have . . . something I . . . want to suggest . . . to you."

"What is it?"

She hesitated before she replied:

"When I was . . . searching for the herbs . . . which I know will help you . . . I felt sure . . . Mama was . . . beside me."

She looked at him quickly, as if she expected him to say something cynical, or at least to show it on his face.

She was, however, reassured, and she went on:

"When I found them . . . I felt that Mama was . . . telling me I must . . . try to heal your eyes as . . . she healed people, in which she was always . . . successful."

Again Erlina waited, as if she expected the Marquis to say it was nonsense and he was not having any part of it.

Instead, he said:

"What do you wish to do?"

"I would like to put my hands over your eyes and pray, as Mama did. But you will have to cooperate in a way which I will explain to you when we do it."

There was a short silence.

"Very well," the Marquis replied. "I agree. In fact, I will agree to anything which will make me see again."

"You will see . . . you will—I know it!" Erlina cried.

She got up from the floor.

"I am going to change," she said, "into one of the lovely gowns I found stored in the attic, and I hope, even though you cannot see me, you will realise I am looking extremely smart, in fact, very unlike myself."

"Now you are speaking exactly like a woman!" the Marquis teased.

Erlina did not answer.

She was so delighted that he had agreed to let her try to heal his eyes that she ran as quickly as she could to her bedroom.

Yesterday, she and Gerry had explored the attics.

The Marquis had been busy talking to a man whom Mr. Cranley had brought to the house.

He was a Farmer who had lost his farm during the war and was longing to get back to the soil.

Erlina and Gerry had gone up to the attics and

found that while the rain had come through in some places, the roofs of the North and South Wings were undamaged.

In the North Wing there were a number of trunks.

When Erlina opened them she found they contained all the clothes that had belonged to the Marquis's Mother. They had been brought from London when she died.

There were six of them filled with gowns, cloaks, furs, and lingerie.

All of them were most exquisite and expensive.

There was also in the attic the clothes which the Marquis had worn when he was a boy.

They had been carefully packed away by the Housekeeper as he grew out of them.

Some of them fitted Gerry perfectly.

He had run downstairs to tell the Marquis as soon as he was free what they had found.

He had agreed to Gerry having anything he required, and gave Erlina the same permission.

"Do you really mean that I can wear those beautiful gowns?" she asked.

"It would be a pity to leave them to rot," the Marquis pointed out.

"It will save me from worrying about my appearance, and also having to ask you for money in advance."

"Of course! You have only one gown!" the Marquis exclaimed. "I should have thought of that myself."

"I have had it for three years, and it is not only threadbare, but also beginning to split at the seams," Erlina confessed.

"The wardrobes in the attics are yours as far as I am concerned," the Marquis said, "and we must ask Cranley to find somebody who can alter the dresses that are too big for you."

"How do you know that I am not bigger and perhaps fatter than your Mother?" Erlina asked.

"I have been working it out for myself," the Marquis answered. "I know that your head is level with my shoulders. I know too that you have been eating very little for some time, so you must be thin. And you are also very light on your feet."

Erlina clapped her hands together.

"That is clever of you!" she said. "And of course you are right."

Now, when she was putting on one of the beautiful gowns which had come from Bond Street, she wished that the Marquis could see her in it and perhaps admire her.

Then she told herself sharply that was something he was very unlikely to do.

He was used to being surrounded by the best dressed and most beautiful women in London.

She was only a country bumpkin.

As she went downstairs, she thought over what the Marquis had said about never marrying.

She knew it was wrong for him to think like that.

Of course he must marry. He must have a son to inherit the title and to live at Meldon Hall.

"Once he has restored it and the Estate is working at full capacity," she told herself, "I feel sure he will want not one son, but several to enjoy it as much as he will."

It suddenly struck her that perhaps he would

want to go back to London.

In which case, once again the place might become as run down as it was now.

"He must not do that . . . he must not!" she told herself.

She wondered how she could encourage him to make it one of the most outstanding estates in the whole country.

As she reached the hall, Dawes came from the direction of the Pantry.

"Luncheon's ready, Miss Erlina!" he announced, "and th' Missus'll be upset if what she's cooked doesn't please His Lordship."

"How have the girls been?" Erlina enquired.

The Vicar, by what seemed to be a miracle, had produced the daughters of one of the families who had been obliged to leave the village.

They had been willing to come back to work at the Hall.

Erlina thought that their food should take priority over the cleaning of the house.

She had, therefore, given both the girls to Mrs. Dawes to help her in the Kitchen.

Once they had arrived, Mrs. Dawes had become a different person.

She looked younger, she laughed, talked incessantly, and was producing the most delicious meals any of them had tasted for years.

Dawes now had a footman, a rather stupid boy, but at least he was a pair of hands.

The Vicar, on his last visit, had said he was looking for another.

'What we want now is housemaids,' Erlina thought as she walked into the room where the Marquis was sitting.

He was talking to Gerry, who had just come from the stables where he had spent most of his time with the horses.

"Luncheon is ready," Erlina said, "and if we are not hungry, Mrs. Dawes will be very disappointed."

"I am very hungry," Gerry replied, "and Mrs. Dawes's food is scrumptious. I shall soon be so fat that I shall need a bigger pair of breeches!"

"They are waiting for you whenever you require them," Erlina replied, "and I hope you remembered to thank His Lordship for letting you have them."

"I thanked him—I did thank you, did I not?" Gerry said to the Marquis.

"Of course you did," the Marquis agreed, "and I hope you look as smart in them as I did when I wore them."

He had risen from his chair and put his hand on Gerry's shoulder.

The boy guided him across the room and through the door into the hall.

Walking behind them, Erlina thought how tall and strong the Marquis looked with his broad shoulders.

As Gerry chatted away happily to him, she told herself again that of course he must have a son.

It was foolish to let his unhappy childhood go on hurting him.

They reached the Dining-Room.

Dawes and the footman had now made it spotlessly clean, and the table was shining like a mirror.

They sat down as they always did, with the Marquis between them.

Gerry went on talking excitedly about the horses and some of the things he had found in the attics.

"Did you know, My Lord, there is a bow and arrow there," he asked, "and several duelling-pistols?"

"You might try shooting with the bow and arrows," the Marquis replied, "but I think you must get a little older before you start duelling!"

"Have you ever fought in a duel?" Erlina asked.

"Yes," the Marquis answered, "and I am delighted to say that I came out the winner."

Erlina was just about to ask him what was the reason for the contest.

She then thought that it had involved a woman.

It would have been a question of who owned her at the end of the duel.

She could understand that the Marquis was delighted he had won.

At the same time, she wondered what the woman had looked like and if she was very lovely.

Perhaps the Marquis had been very happy with her.

Then she told herself that was all in the past, and anyway it would be a great mistake to question him about his private life.

When luncheon was over, Gerry went off to the stables again, and the Marquis said to Erlina:

"Now, what are we going to do?"

"You know . . . what I . . . want," she answered.

"Very well," he answered, "I am in your hands. Where shall we go?"

"I want to take you to the Music Room," Erlina replied. "I discovered it only yesterday, and besides being a beautiful room with windows that open onto the garden, it actually contains a very fine piano."

She started to lead the Marquis down the corridor.

"Now I think of it," he said, "just before my Mother died I remember her buying a Broadwood Grand. I suppose it must have been for here rather than for London."

"It is a Broadwood that I found," Erlina said, "and it is very thrilling because it is one with the iron tension bars which not many people have yet seen."

"Are you telling me in some obscure way," the Marquis asked, "that you play the piano?"

"Of course I do," Erlina replied, "but whether you will enjoy what I play is quite a different matter."

"I think I should warn you that I am very critical," the Marquis said teasingly.

"That is what I expected," she rejoined.

They reached the Music Room.

Erlina glanced at the piano which was standing on a dais.

It was, she thought, the most precious thing in the room and something she would love to own herself.

For the moment, however, she had to think about the Marquis.

She led him to the long french windows which opened onto the garden.

By now the sun was very hot, but there was a

faint breeze blowing over the neglected lawns and flower-beds, which had run wild.

Erlina had told Dawes what she intended to do, and he had lowered the sun-blind over the windows.

It was faded and torn at the edges but could still keep the sun from entering the Music Room.

There was a comfortable armchair facing the window.

Erlina led the Marquis to it and said:

"Your chair is in front of you. When you sit down you will feel the cool air coming through the trees and smell the flowers that are just outside."

She paused a moment and then continued:

"I expect you remember the rose garden with the sun dial in the centre of it, which I am sure is very old."

The Marquis did not answer, but lowered himself carefully onto the chair.

When he wanted to stretch out his legs, Erlina brought a low stool and placed it under his feet.

"What happens now?" he asked.

She thought there was a slightly hostile note in his voice, as if he resented being so helpless.

"Now you have to help me," Erlina said softly, "and you must remember that while my Mother taught me what to do, I have never done this before without her being there."

The Marquis did not reply, and she went on:

"I want you to relax and think that you are seeing a light, a vivid light, pouring down upon you and especially penetrating your eyes. Do not think of anything else—just the light coming from the sky."

As she spoke, she moved behind the chair.

Bending forward, she put her hands very gently over the black bandage which covered the Marquis's eyes.

She could feel his skin under her little finger and thumb of each hand. Her other fingers rested on the bandage.

Then she prayed, as her Mother had taught her, that the Life Force would pour through her hands and bring the Marquis back his sight.

She did not know how long she prayed.

She felt as if she poured her whole being towards him.

She gave him the life force from herself as well as from the dazzling light, which she believed he was receiving from Heaven.

Then she took her hands from his eyes, and without speaking walked towards the piano.

She sat down on the stool.

She thought at this moment no music she knew was appropriate for what she was feeling and what she hoped the Marquis felt too.

Instead, she played as she had often improvised to herself.

It was the music of the woods, the flowers, the birds singing in the trees, and the fish swimming in the clear stream.

Only after she had played for perhaps a quarter of an hour did she feel as if she had become herself again.

She was no longer being carried away as she had been while she was trying to heal the Marquis.

She stopped playing and was still for a moment with her hands resting in her lap.

Then she rose and walked to his chair.

She thought at first he was asleep, but as she stood looking down at him, the Marquis said:

"Thank you, Erlina! I feel sure your prayers, if nothing else, have helped me."

"Do you ... mean ... that? Do you ... really mean ... it?"

"I would not tell you anything but the truth," he replied. "The truth is that while I knew you were praying for me, and while I tried to see the light you told me to look for, I did not know—how could I know?—whether if my eyes were unbandaged I would see any more than I could before you tried to heal me."

"You cannot expect miracles the first time I try," Erlina answered, "and I want ... you to let me ... try again."

"You may try as often as you like," the Marquis said, "and I enjoyed the way you were telling me what is happening in my woods, my gardens, and my stream."

Erlina stared at him. Then she gave a little cry.

"How did you know I was telling you that?"

"I knew that was what you were playing."

"Now you are ... really beginning to look with your heart," Erlina said. "Do you think you would have known what I was saying to you in prayer a month ago?"

"I suppose you are right," the Marquis said ruefully, "and I am using my perception in a way I have not used it before."

"Of course you are," Erlina said as she smiled, "and please, may I ask you if I can do something else?"

"What is that?" the Marquis enquired.

"Can I . . . when you are in the dark, try to heal your eyes when you are not . . . wearing your . . . bandages?"

For a moment she thought the Marquis was going to refuse, then he said:

"All right. You can come to my room when I am ready for bed and Hignet removes my bandage. Do you really think it will make any difference if you actually touch my eyes."

"Yes, I do," Erlina declared, "and thank you, thank you! I know that what I am trying to do will be more effective if I can actually touch you with my fingers."

She stood for a moment, feeling emotional at the thought.

Then she walked out through the window onto the terrace, which bordered the Rose-Garden.

"Why have you left me?" the Marquis asked.

"I am just thinking," Erlina replied, "that very soon you will be able to see how beautiful the roses are despite having had no attention, and the lawn wants cutting, but it is still very green."

"We must have some gardeners," the Marquis said sharply.

The way he spoke awoke Erlina from the dream she had moved in ever since she had prayed for the Marquis.

She turned back.

"Yes, of course we must," she agreed. "But housing must have priority, and as you told the workmen to restore the Vicarage first, they have only just started on one of the cottages."

"Why can we not employ more men?" the

Marquis enquired. "They tell me there is a lot of unemployment, and I am sure that men who have been discharged from the Army and Navy can easily turn their hands to carpentry and painting."

"I know that Mr. Cranley is trying to engage all the ex-servicemen he can," Erlina said, "and those I have spoken to who are working on the roof are thrilled to be getting employment with such high wages."

She knew the Marquis had been very generous in what he had promised those who were starting on the restoration.

But it was dificult for him, Erlina thought, because he could not see to realise how much work there was to be done.

Everything had deteriorated so appallingly in the years when he had abandoned his home.

It was wonderful for her to see the Vicar so happy, Mr. Cranley looking a new man, and the house gradually losing its dust and dirt.

Some of the windows had been cleaned, and the difference between them and those that had not was an incentive to everybody to go on working.

It was like watching a transformation scene, Erlina thought.

She had never actually seen one performed, but she had read about them in some of the books that described the operas that had been staged in Vienna.

She could imagine how exciting and moving it would be, even when one knew it was all part of an act.

But to see it in real life, as she was watching

Meldon Hall being restored to its original splendour, was very moving.

"Come and sit down to talk to me," the Marquis commanded. "I am bored with doing nothing, and I am thinking perhaps tomorrow I will go riding."

Erlina gave a cry of horror.

"Of course you cannot do that! It would be far too dangerous! And however careful we were, it would be terrible if you had a fall and did any more damage to your eyes!"

"I must have some exercise," the Marquis complained.

"You can exercise yourself morning and evening in your bedroom," Erlina replied, "and of course you can walk in the garden, and I will be very careful not to let you slip or fall down."

"Dammit all!" the Marquis swore fiercely. "I am a man, not a puppet!"

Erlina did not speak. He said in a contrite voice:

"I apologise for my language, but it makes me so angry to have to sit here and not be able to do anything. My horses are in the stables and only Gerry can enjoy himself riding them."

"It is very kind of you to let him do so," Erlina said. "At the same time, we have to look after you and protect you."

"That is what I should be saying to you," the Marquis retorted.

"Perhaps you will be able to in a short time," Erlina said.

She thought as she spoke that if the Marquis regained his sight, he would probably not want to protect her, but somebody very different.

Even as she thought it, there was the sound of

the door of the Music Room opening.

Then she was aware that two people were coming towards them.

She turned round and stared.

First she saw a tall, very fashionably dressed young man.

With him was a lady who she realised at once was exceedingly beautiful.

She was also arranged in silk, satin, feathers, and diamonds. Erlina thought she could not be real.

The man walked towards the Marquis and said:

"At last, we have found you, Michael! What in the name of Heaven made you come down here, of all places?"

"So it is you, Oliver!" the Marquis remarked. "I cannot think how you managed to find me."

"I used my brain, my dear Cousin," the man called Oliver said, "and when I at last knew where you were, I of course came to cheer you up, bringing Isabel with me."

The Lady moved forward as the Marquis's Cousin spoke, and bent down to kiss him lightly on the cheek.

"I am very angry with you, my Dearest, most Beloved Michael," she said, "for not telling me where you were going! You know I would have come with you."

"I wanted no one with me," the Marquis replied.

He spoke disagreeably.

His Cousin Oliver and the Beauty, wearing a bonnet decorated with flame-coloured ostrich feathers, stared at Erlina.

"And who is this?" Oliver enquired coldly.

"I should have introduced you," the Marquis replied, "to Miss Erlina Sherwood, whose Estate marches with this, and who, most unfortunately, has just had her home burnt to the ground."

"That is indeed a disaster!" Oliver remarked.

"Erlina," the Marquis went on, "allow me to introduce my Cousin—Oliver Mell—and Lady Isabel Fisher."

Erlina curtsied and, while Oliver Mell bowed, she was aware that Lady Isabel looked at her with hostile eyes.

"I cannot imagine," she said softly to the Marquis, "why you did not send for me when you arrived home. After all, it is I who should be looking after you and keeping you happy."

"I had no wish to see anyone," the Marquis retorted.

"Except, it seems, Miss Sherwood!" Lady Isabel murmured.

"Miss Sherwood is helping me restore the house and the Estate to what it was before I neglected it," the Marquis explained.

"Good Heavens!" his Cousin Oliver exclaimed. "You told me you would never set foot in Meldon Hall again! That is why it was the last place I looked for you."

"I changed my mind," the Marquis said shortly. "Until I got here I did not realise what damage I had done by refusing to come home. Now, somewhat belatedly, I am trying to put things to rights."

"Which of course is a wonderful idea of yours," Lady Isabel said, "and you know, Dearest Michael, that I will help in every way I can."

She spoke in a cooing, seductive voice.

Listening, Erlina had the feeling that it somehow did not ring true.

She thought, too, and she was sure she was not mistaken, that Oliver Mell was not as fond of his Cousin as he was pretending to be.

Feeling somewhat embarrassed by the way they were both looking at her, she said to the Marquis:

"If your guests are staying to tea, My Lord, I will go and arrange for it to be served in the Drawing-Room, or would you prefer it here?"

"Staying for tea?" Oliver Mell protested. "We have brought our trunks with us, and also our servants. We are going to look after you, Michael, as we would have done if you had not disappeared immediately after your accident."

Erlina saw the Marquis's lips tighten, as if he was trying to prevent himself from saying that he did not want them here.

Feeling the situation was somewhat uncomfortable, Erlina walked towards the door.

"I will arrange for tea in the Drawing-Room," she said.

As she shut the door behind her, she heard Oliver Mell say:

"Trust you, Michael, to have some beautiful creature around to alleviate your suffering. At the same time, is it not a little indiscreet?"

Erlina did not wait to hear the Marquis's reply, but ran down the corridor towards the hall.

Dawes was there, and she said to him:

"I think we had better have tea in the Drawing-Room."

"That's what I thinks you'd want, Miss Erlina," Dawes replied.

As he spoke, Hignet came through the green baize door.

"Wot's all this?" he asked. "I've jest bin told that Mr. Oliver's here, and that's bad news!"

"Why do you say that?" Erlina questioned.

"Cos them Cousins ain't never got on, Miss," Hignet replied. "In fact, 'twere Mr. Oliver as arranged th' Steeple-Chase in which 'Is Lordship were injured."

"They have come to stay," Erlina said.

"Not if 'Is Lordship c'n 'elp it!" Hignet retorted. " 'E might 'ave to 'ave them here for th' night, 'cause they've brought a whole crowd with 'em."

Erlina looked concerned.

"How many?" she asked.

"From what I 'ears from th' men as is workin' in th' Kitchens, there be a coachman, a footman, two Outriders, 'is Valet and 'Er Ladyship's maid, 'sides two on th' Brake."

Erlina put up her hands in horror.

"How are we to accommodate so many?" she asked. "Even if they wait on themselves, Mrs. Dawes will not be able to cook for them all."

Hignet thought for a moment.

Then he said:

"I thinks, Miss, it'd be sensible to say you'll accommodate Mr. Oliver's Valet and 'Er Ladyship's maid for th' night, but all th' rest'll 'ave to go to th' nearest Posting Inn. There be one in t' next village."

"Yes, I know that," Erlina said, "but it seems very inhospitable."

"Don't you worry 'bout that," Hignet said. "Mr. Oliver's bin living off 'Is Lordship for years! 'E pleads fer money as if 'e 'xpects it t' fall like manna from 'Eaven!"

Erlina gave a choked laugh.

At the same time, she knew it would be impossible to have so many people staying in the house when they were not yet ready for it.

"I do not know how I can tell His Lordship what you suggest," she said at length.

"Leave it ter me," Hignet said. " 'E'll know its fer the best an' yer can't work miracles."

"Then please tell him that you suggested it," Erlina said, "and I will go and help Mrs. Dawes with the tea."

She went towards the Kitchen.

As she did so, she was thinking that the newcomers had swept away the peace and happiness she had found since coming to Meldon Hall.

Now she was uncertain of herself and afraid of making mistakes and, most of all, of upsetting the Marquis.

She was sure in her heart that her healing had done some good to his eyes.

But he could certainly not be upset or worried.

If, as Hignet had said, he did not get on with his Cousin, then Oliver Mell was the last person she wanted at the Hall.

Hignet had said it was Oliver Mell who was responsible for the Marquis's accident.

If so, he was certainly not welcome while the Marquis was still blind.

"Oh, why did they have to come?" she asked.

"Why did they have to spoil everything?"

Then she told herself it was bound to happen sooner or later.

The Marquis might have tried to escape from the outside world.

But the outside world had come to him.

chapter five

BY the time tea was ready, Erlina had helped
Mrs. Dawes to produce what was an attractive
meal.

There were sandwiches, scones, and hot
buttered toast.

Besides a number of little cakes, there was a
large sultana cake, which Mrs. Dawes was an
expert at making.

Hignet had helped, then Erlina asked him to
go to tell the Marquis and his guests that tea was
ready.

"I 'opes 'Is Lordship's gettin' rid o' them, that's
wot I 'opes," Hignet said. "You can bet your last
penny as Mr. Oliver'll be scheming to get some
more money out o' him."

"Why should the Marquis be so generous to
him?" Erlina asked.

"Mr. Oliver be his Heir Presumptive," Hignet replied.

"Heir Presumptive?" Erlina exclaimed. "Do you mean that if the Marquis does not have a son, he will inherit the title and the Estate?"

"That's right, Miss," Hignet said, "an' it'd be a disaster—that's wot that'd be—a real disaster!"

As he spoke, he walked away towards the Music Room.

Erlina looked at him with concern in her eyes.

If the Marquis did not have a son, then Oliver Mell would come into the Estate.

She was certain from what she felt, as well as from what Hignet had said, that he was a bad man.

If he were to inherit the Estate things would then be as bad, if not worse, than they were now.

She perceived that he would not wish to live in the country, and would spend all his money in London.

"I must persuade the Marquis that he must get married and have a son," she told herself.

The terrifying question then rose again—what would happen to Gerry and her?

The party came into the Drawing-Room and Lady Isabel looked, Erlina thought, somewhat disdainfully at the food.

She also spoke to Erlina in a sharp voice.

It was very different from the cooing, dulcet tones with which she spoke to the Marquis.

Erlina had just poured out the tea, when Gerry came running into the room.

"What do you think, My Lord," he said

impulsively to the Marquis before he noticed the newcomers, "there are new horses in the stables, eight of them, but they are not as fine as yours."

Then he saw that the Marquis was not alone with his sister.

"Who is this, Michael?" Oliver asked in a suspicious voice. "I did not know you had opened the Hall to children."

The Marquis replied, speaking in the supercilious and cold tone which he had not used for some days.

"Let me introduce you," he said, "to Sir Gerald Sherwood. He is the Sixth Baronet and, as I have already told you, owns the Estate which marches with mine."

As Gerry had been well trained by Erlina, he held out his hand first to Lady Isabel, then to Oliver Mell.

"How do you do," he said. "I have been talking to your horses."

"I only wish they were mine," Oliver Mell replied, "but actually the horses you were disparaging belong to His Lordship."

"They are mine?" the Marquis asked sharply.

"We did not think Isabel's team was as good as yours, so I borrowed the bays and your carriage in which to bring her here."

"You did not drive them yourself?" the Marquis enquired.

Oliver Mell gave a somewhat contrived laugh.

"No, Jackson would not let me, so he has come with them, but I have also brought down *Titus,* the horse you wished to buy from me. I thought it would please you, as you were in the country."

"I would have liked to see him first," the Marquis said, "but as you have brought him with you, I suppose I must keep my word and give you a thousand pounds for him."

Oliver Mell smiled.

"That is exactly what I require at the moment," he said, "and I suppose you would not like to make it ten, and get me out of the hands of the Dunns?"

"We have discussed this before," the Marquis replied, "and I have not altered my decision."

Oliver Mell shrugged his shoulders, and walked away to the window.

Erlina felt the situation was uncomfortable and very bad for the Marquis.

As if she felt the same, Lady Isabel moved to sit down beside him on the sofa.

"You are not to trouble your head over Oliver's difficulties," she said softly. "I have been so concerned over you, Dearest Michael, that it has been impossible to think of anything else."

The Marquis did not reply.

Erlina, having poured out the tea, thought that she and Gerry should leave.

She piled a plate with a number of small sandwiches, cakes, and scones and said to Gerry:

"Come with me. There is something I want to talk to you about."

He was eating a sandwich and looked at her in surprise.

Erlina turned to Lady Isabel.

"I am sure, My Lady, you will be kind enough to

pour His Lordship another cup of tea, if he wants one?"

"You can be quite certain of that," Lady Isabel said tartly, "and kindly see to it that my maid is looked after and my trunks unpacked."

"There is no need to unpack too much," the Marquis interposed. "I am afraid we cannot accommodate you more than for just tonight. The house is not yet ready to receive guests."

Lady Isabel gave a shrill cry.

"Michael! How can you be so unkind when I have come so far just to see you, and to help you get well."

"I need no one's help but Miss Sherwood's," the Marquis replied. "She knows exactly what to do."

"If you send us back tomorrow," Oliver Mell said slowly, turning round from the window, "I think it will be too much of a strain to put on your horses. We came here in a hurry, and spent only one night on the road."

The Marquis was silent, and Erlina saw he was frowning.

Then he said:

"Very well, you will stay for two nights and leave on Wednesday. It may seem inhospitable, but as I told you, I wish to be alone, and the Doctors' orders are that I must have complete quiet, and on no account should I be upset."

"Then, of course, Dearest Michael," Lady Isabel cooed, "we will do whatever pleases you. At the same time, I cannot imagine how I could upset you in any way."

The Marquis did not reply to this, and Erlina walked towards the door.

"I will go and see about the rooms," she said, "and talk to Mrs. Dawes about dinner."

Somewhat reluctantly Gerry followed her, but then stopped to say to the Marquis:

"The stables are overcrowded. Some of the horses will have to go into the paddock."

He did not wait to her the Marquis's reply, but ran after Erlina.

She took him into the small Sitting-Room on the other side of the hall and gave him the plate she was carrying.

"We do not want all these people here," Gerry said, "and the coachmen and grooms were all grumbling and saying there is hardly room 'to swing a cat'!"

Erlina knew that a good part of the stables was uninhabitable.

She could understand that the men found it irritating.

She had a great deal to do, however, and left Gerry to go to the Kitchen.

Hignet was there, and he said as she appeared:

"Now, don't you fuss yourself, Miss. Everythin's under control an' th' lot from London's gone off already to th' Postin'-Inn."

Erlina sighed in relief. Hignet went on:

"'Cept fer Jackson. 'E be one o' us, so to speak, so he be stayin' here. I'll find a room for 'im."

"The Marquis has told his Cousin they are to leave on Wednesday," Erlina said.

"That be two nights," Mrs. Dawes said. "There's nobody to make up their beds an' do their rooms."

"I have been thinking about that," Erlina said. "Her Ladyship's maid can look after hers, and perhaps Hignet will be kind enough to give me a hand with first cleaning hers and then Mr. Oliver's."

"I just knowed it would be me!" Hignet said in mock dismay.

But he was smiling, and Erlina knew he would not let her down.

They got rooms ready on the same floor as theirs.

Hignet thought it would be right to use the State Rooms.

As Erlina had not been able to get any housemaids yet, the rooms were very dusty.

All they could do in such a short time was to brush the carpet and dust the dressing-table and other furniture.

As they did so, Erlina said to Hignet despairingly:

"How could I have imagined that visitors would arrive before we had time to do anything but clean the downstairs rooms?"

"'Tis always th' same," Hignet answered. "Women be like bees round a 'oney-pot where 'Is Lordship's concerned."

There was a little silence, then Erlina remarked.

"I expect he enjoys that . . . as any man would."

"They never lasts long," Hignet said, "an' if yer asks me, 'Er Ladyship be on th' way out."

Erlina thought it was incorrect for her to ask any more questions.

They went from Lady Isabel's room, and started to clean what they could of the one that was to be occupied by Oliver Mell.

As she thought about him and what Hignet had said, she felt sure he would upset the Marquis.

Therefore, the sooner he left, the better.

There was, however, nothing she could do about it.

It was only by a tremendous effort that she had the room at least habitable by the time she had to dress for dinner, since Hignet had to leave her to look after the Marquis.

She saw the Marquis coming up the stairs with Hignet and hurried to meet him as he reached the top.

"I believe, My Lord," she said, "it would be easier if you had dinner alone with your guests tonight. You will not want Gerry and me with you."

The Marquis had stopped still when she spoke to him, and now he said:

"You are in charge of the house, Erlina, and I expect you and your brother to dine with me as you have always done. I will not have people who drop in unexpectedly upsetting my arrangements."

He sounded annoyed, and Erlina felt it would be a mistake to argue with him.

She, therefore, said nothing.

He walked on down to the end of the corridor to the Master Suite.

She went into Gerry's room, and found him playing with the bow and arrows he had brought down from the attic.

"The Vicar has put up a target for Tom and me," he said. "I shot four bull's-eyes today and Tom got only two!"

"That was very satisfactory," Erlina said, "and when we have time, we can see if there are some more things up there which will amuse you both."

The Vicar had arranged that Gerry and Tom should have lessons together, starting next week.

"You cannot expect them not to want to explore everything on the Estate first," he said to Erlina, "and they will work hard to make up for lost time."

"I think that is sensible," Erlina agreed, "and it would be difficult at the moment to keep them out of the stables."

She had arranged for her brother and Tom to ride every morning.

That they were mounted on the Marquis's horses was an inexpressible delight to both boys.

She, therefore, understood when Gerry asked:

"Why did those people have to come here? We do not want them."

"They are staying only until Wednesday," Erlina said, "and you must be very polite to them because they are friends of His Lordship."

"I do not think His Lordship wants them," Gerry said perceptively.

Erlina thought she should not contradict or agree with him.

Instead, she kissed his cheek and said:

"We must just make them as comfortable as we can. Now, hurry up and change for dinner. And do not forget, go to bed as soon as the meal is finished without my telling you."

"I will not forget," Gerry said, "but I would rather talk to His Lordship than that other man."

Erlina went to her own room.

She could not help being feminine enough to resent Lady Isabel's hostility.

She, therefore, chose to wear at dinner one of the prettiest gowns she had brought down from the attic.

It was a little too big for her, but fortunately fashion had decreed there should be no waist.

The skirt fell from under the bust.

It was decorated with satin flowers round the hem and on the puffed sleeves.

Erlina did not like to think how much it must have cost.

She knew that neither she nor her Mother had ever owned such an expensive gown.

It was fortunate that the Marchioness had bought so many things shortly before she died.

The fashions too had changed very little in the years after the war, the exception being that gowns had become more elaborate.

She was, therefore, not surprised when Lady Isabel entered the Drawing-Room wearing a very elaborately decorated gown.

It did not, however, in any way eclipse the one Erlina was wearing.

She thought Lady Isabel looked surprised at her appearance as she said sharply:

"I thought from what His Lordship said that your house had been burned down."

"It has been," Erlina replied, "but luckily I have something to wear."

Lady Isabel looked at her suspiciously.

"Your gown certainly came from Bond Street," she remarked, "and you must be very rich to afford one of *Madame* Rachel's models!"

Erlina did not have to answer for at that moment the Marquis came into the room.

He had been guided down the stairs by Gerry.

"Oh, here you are, Dearest Michael!" Lady Isabel gushed.

She walked across the room and kissed him on the cheek.

"It is so lovely to be here with you," she said.

Then, in what might have been *sotto voce* but was perfectly audible to Erlina, she asked:

"Surely that child is not dining with us?"

"Gerry is my guest, just as you are," the Marquis said, "and we have dinner early because it suits Mrs. Dawes, my Cook."

Watching her, Erlina saw Lady Isabel look at Gerry in the same hostile way as she had at her.

But she was too sensible to say anything.

Oliver came into the room, and they moved in to dinner, Gerry again guiding the Marquis at his request.

Erlina had thought that perhaps the Marquis would not want to eat with so many people present.

She remembered how he had made an exception of having her and Gerry with him when they had first come to the Hall.

It then became apparent as the meal

progressed that he had arranged everything with Hignet.

The food that was put in front of him had already been cut up.

There were no sauces or gravy which would have made his eating messy.

Because Erlina thought she should not push herself forward, she was silent while Lady Isabel talked exclusively to the Marquis.

Oliver Mell was at first silent.

Then, after he had drunk a considerable amount of wine, he became more voluble.

"Tell me about yourself, Miss Sherwood," he said, "and why you waste your beauty on the turnips instead of coming to London?"

"The answer to that is quite simple," Erlina replied. "We had little money when the war ended, and I had my Father's Estate to look after."

"Now your house has been burned down," Oliver said, "you must come to London, where I prophesize you will be a great success."

He lowered his voice as he added:

"It cannot be very amusing for you here."

"On the contrary, I am very content to help His Lordship restore his house and the village, and of course, to get back his sight."

"Do you think that is possible?" Oliver Mell asked in a whisper.

"I am quite certain it is," Erlina replied firmly.

She had the feeling that was not the answer Oliver Mell wanted.

She thought as the dinner progressed that

there was something about him that was distinctly unpleasant.

She could not explain it even to herself.

But she knew she was right in thinking that his only motive for seeking out his Cousin was to extract money from him.

He was also hoping—although she felt it must be just her imagination—that he would remain blind.

When dinner was over, they all moved into the Drawing-Room, with the gentlemen not remaining behind.

Erlina thought she would retire.

She was just about to say that she would go upstairs with Gerry, when the Marquis said:

"I am tired, as I am sure you must be, Isabel, after such a long drive, and I suggest we all go to bed early."

"You are quite right, Dearest Michael, as you always are," Lady Isabel answered, "and I am definitely fatigued. I have always disliked the swaying of a carriage."

She paused before she added:

"And of course, Dearest, there is always to-morrow when we can be together, and I have a great deal to say to you."

The Marquis did not answer.

He only rose to his feet.

As if he had ordered him to do so, Gerry went to his side.

The Marquis put his hand on Gerry's shoulder and started to walk towards the door.

Isabel gave a little cry.

"You did not say good-night to me—unless you

would like me to come and see you a little later?"

She said the last few words in a low voice, but Erlina heard them clearly.

"Certainly not!" the Marquis replied quickly. "I wish to sleep, Isabel, and I suggest you do the same."

He paused a moment and then continued:

"Good-night, and if the beds are uncomfortable it is really your own fault. Naturally we are not yet ready to accommodate visitors, and shall not be for several months."

He did not wait for a reply, but went out through the door with Gerry.

Erlina was aware that Lady Isabel was looking at Oliver Mell.

At the same time, she made a little gesture with her hands as if she thought the situation was hopeless.

Leaving them both looking somewhat nonplussed, Erlina hurried after the Marquis and Gerry.

Only as she reached the door did she hear Lady Isabel say:

"Do you think Michael paid for that gown?"

Erlina caught up with the Marquis, and they went slowly up the stairs.

"How have you managed to accommodate them?" he asked. "I thought we had no one to help clean the rooms."

"The Vicar has found a housemaid who is coming next week," Erlina replied, "and Mr. Cranley has heard of one at Boxstead who he is interviewing to-morrow. In the meantime, Hignet and I have done our best."

"I hope to God nobody else finds out where I am," the Marquis said. "I do not wish to be seen, and I do not want to be talked about! All I want is to be left alone!"

"Except for us," Gerry said. "You do want us, don't you, My Lord?"

There was an anxious note in his voice, which was very obvious.

"Of course I want you," the Marquis replied. "Who else would lead me about as well as you do? Who else would take such good care of my horses?"

"I helped the grooms rub down two horses this morning," Gerry boasted, "and they said I did it very well."

"I am sure you did," the Marquis said as he smiled.

They reached the Master Suite and Erlina saw that Hignet was there.

"Come on, M'Lord," he said. "What you wants is rest."

"I am sick of resting, and I am sick of being blind!" the Marquis exploded.

He spoke petulantly, like a child.

"Do not forget you have Eyebright and Fennel to help you," Erlina said. "They are very important."

"I will not forget," the Marquis promised, "and thank you, Erlina."

He turned round to put his hand for a moment on her arm.

Then he patted Gerry on the head.

"I have a secret to tell you to-morrow morning," he said.

"A secret!" Gerry exclaimed. "That is exciting!"

"I think that is what you will find it," the Marquis answered.

Hignet led him in through the door, and Erlina went with Gerry to his room.

"I wonder what is the secret he is going to tell me," Gerry said.

"If it is a secret, you must not tell anyone," Erlina replied, "not even Tom, unless he says you may."

"I hope it is a really scrumptious secret, all for me!"

Erlina helped him undress, heard his prayers, and tucked him up in bed.

It had been a long day and he was very sleepy.

"Good-night, Erlina," he said as she kissed him. "It is . . . fun being . . . here!"

"Great fun!" she agreed.

She kissed him again, blew out the candle beside his bed, and went to the door.

"God and His Angels watch over you, Darling," she whispered as she reached it.

She thought as she went down the corridor that he was already half-asleep, and had not heard her.

She went to her own room.

She sat down at the French *Sécretaire* that was in a corner of the room.

She began to make a list of all the things that would be required tomorrow.

She knew, with the visitors, that Mrs. Dawes

would want a lot more things from the shops in the next village.

She decided to send one of the Outriders early in the morning to collect them.

She then undressed, and was just brushing her hair, when there came a knock on her door.

She thought it might be Lady Isabel's lady's-maid.

Quickly she put on her negligee and opened the door.

It was Hignet who stood there.

"If yer ain't gone to bed, Miss," he said, "'Is Lordship'd like yer to do 'is eyes."

"Do his eyes?" Erlina repeated in surprise.

"'E said you wanted to do them wi'out a bandage on."

"Yes, yes . . . of course," Erlina answered, "but I did not think tonight . . ."

"It's what 'e wants," Hignet said, "an' as yer knows, Miss, we 'as to give in to 'im."

"Y-yes . . . of course," Erlina agreed.

"'E's told me what yer said," Hignet went on, "an' I've put a chair fer 'im close beside the bed so that when you finish 'e can get into 'is bed wi'out any 'elp."

Erlina nodded to show she understood.

"But if 'e goes to sleep in it, it won't matter. He'll be comfortable in the chair with his feet up an' I've put a blanket over 'is legs so's 'e won't be cold."

"You have thought of everything," Erlina said, "and he is in the dark?"

"Black as pitch, it be," Hignet said, "an' I've

took off 'is bandage, so all you has to do is to go straight to 'is chair."

"I will come at once," Erlina said.

They walked down the corridor.

"Did His Lordship bathe his eyes?" Erlina asked.

"Before dinner an' just now," Hignet answered. "Jest as yer says, Miss, an' there were Fennel in with 'is vegetables."

"That is splendid!" Erlina exclaimed.

The outer door of the Master Suite opened into a small *entre salle,* in which there were two more doors.

One, Erlina knew, led into the bedroom, the other into a *Boudoir.*

"Don't tell 'Is Lordship," Hignet whispered, "or 'e'll be upset at me molly-coddlin' 'im, but I be sleepin' on th' sofa in there."

He winked as he added:

"I'll stop anybody disturbin' 'im."

Erlina was still.

It had never struck her that perhaps Lady Isabel might go to the Marquis in the night.

She was sure it was something he did not want at the moment.

Hignet was right in thinking he should guard him like a watchful sentry.

They reached the Marquis's door, and when Hignet opened it, Erlina could see a very faint light coming through the slightly open door of the *Boudoir.*

"Miss Sherwood, M'Lord," Hignet announced. "I told 'er where you'd be."

Erlina stepped into the darkness.

She just had a glimpse of the back of a chair.

Hignet shut the door, and the room was completely dark.

She stood behind the Marquis's chair and said softly:

"You know what to do. Think of a light shining down from Heaven, and I will try then to make some light pour from me into your eyes."

The Marquis did not answer.

She put out her hands and very gently found his head lying back against a pillow.

It was in exactly the right position for her to put both her hands over his eyes.

The middle fingers of each hand were on the lids themselves.

It gave her a strange feeling to touch his skin.

She knew without his saying anything that he was upset at the arrival of his Cousin and Lady Isabel.

He was unable to relax as he had done when she had treated him in the afternoon.

Without explaining why, she took her hands from his eyes and started to massage his forehead.

She moved her fingers rhythmically until she felt him respond to their gentleness, and he was no longer tense.

She prayed as she moved her fingers up and down on his forehead.

Finally, she moved them back onto his eyes.

Now she could feel that he had relaxed, and was thinking of the light shining down from the sky.

She was praying as her Mother had taught her to do.

She prayed and prayed, believing that the life force was pouring into him through her fingers.

A long time later she realised he was asleep.

She could feel him breathing steadily, and as she took her fingers away he did not move.

She knew then that he had fallen into a deep and healing sleep.

She walked silently across the room in her bedroom slippers.

At the door she turned the handle without making a noise.

She was not surprised to see that the door of the *Boudoir* was open.

As she closed the Marquis's door Hignet appeared.

She put her finger to her lips to show him that the Marquis was asleep, and he nodded.

Without speaking he opened the door into the corridor, and she slipped through it.

As she moved away, she heard the slight 'click' which told her that Hignet had locked the door behind her.

She had nearly reached her own room, guided by the light of two candles left burning in the silver sconces—she guessed that Hignet had left them burning since there were two newcomers in the house—when suddenly she heard the door of the state room opposite hers opening, which was where Lady Isabel was sleeping.

She came out with her dark hair streaming over her shoulders.

She was wearing a flame-coloured negligee

decorated with lace and velvet bows.

When she saw Erlina she started, then said angrily:

"Where have you been? What were you doing with His Lordship?"

"His Lordship is asleep," Erlina answered. "I have been treating his eyes."

"At this time of night? Do you really expect me to believe such nonsense?" Lady Isabel retorted. "I am not a complete fool!"

"It happens to be true," Erlina said quietly.

"Treating his eyes in your nightgown?" Lady Isabel snarled. "You think because he cannot see you that you have caught him!"

The way she spoke was so offensive that Erlina thought it would be a mistake to reply.

She merely turned to her own door.

As she touched the handle, Lady Isabel came nearer to her.

"Now, listen to me," she said. "If you think you can take His Lordship from me, you are very much mistaken! He is mine, you understand— mine!"

She almost spat the last word and sounded so aggressive that, instinctively, Erlina shrank away from her.

"You may well be frightened," Lady Isabel said, "because I warn you that I will scratch out your eyes! I might even kill you if you come between Michael and me!"

"I have no intention of doing anything of the sort, My Lady," Erlina replied, "and you are entirely mistaken in what you are insinuating in this extremely unpleasant manner."

Lady Isabel laughed, and it was an ugly sound.

"You do not deceive me with that sort of talk," she said, "when I find you slipping in and out of His Lordship's bedroom! Just you get out of this house and stay out! I will look after His Lordship, and nobody like you is going to stop me!"

Erlina opened her bedroom door.

"I think that is for His Lordship to decide for himself," she said. "As I have just told Your Ladyship, you are quite wrong in what you are insinuating in what I consider is a very vulgar manner."

Lady Isabel gave a scream of anger.

But Erlina, as she finished speaking, had gone into her bedroom and closed the door behind her.

She turned the key in the lock.

She was aware that for a few seconds Lady Isabel did not move.

Then she heard her walk away down the corridor.

Erlina knew that she was going to the Marquis's bedroom.

She thought with satisfaction that Hignet had anticipated this and locked the outer door.

Even so, she was afraid that in some way Lady Isabel might manage to wake the Marquis and upset him.

She stood just inside her bedroom, listening.

For what seemed to her a long time, there was silence.

Then she heard Lady Isabel's bedroom door being closed sharply.

With a feeling of triumph, she knew that Lady Isabel had been frustrated in her efforts to reach the Marquis.

She had lost the first move in the battle!

chapter six

ERLINA came back into the house from the stables.

She had gone riding very early in the morning with Gerry and Tom.

It had been a joy to be on a magnificent horse and she and the boys had loved every minute of the ride.

She had also taken the opportunity to look at the horse which Oliver Mell wanted to sell to the Marquis.

It was a fine horse, but she thought personally that a thousand pounds was too much for it.

She knew that Gentlemen did pay large sums at Tattersall's Sale Rooms.

Yet, she was sure her Father would have considered it was worth only half of what he was asking for it.

She had no intention, however, of interfering in what were the Marquis's private affairs, or even offering him her opinion about it.

As she came into the hall, and the boys ran to the Breakfast-Room, Dawes said:

"His Lordship's asking for you, Miss. He's in th' Study with Mr. Oliver."

"I suppose we are rather late," Erlina said contritely, "but it was such a lovely morning!"

"And 'tis good that you can be ridin' one of His Lordship's horses," Dawes added.

Erlina looked at him.

She knew he understood how slow poor old *Nobby* was.

Also, their other horses had not only grown older, but had also become weak from not having the right food.

She took off her riding-hat, and put it on a chair in the hall.

She was wearing a very smart habit which had belonged to the Marchioness.

It was, however, rather elaborate for the country.

Underneath it Her Ladyship had worn a stiffly starched petticoat with a wide hem of real lace.

It was certainly very much more elegant than anything Erlina had ever possessed.

She felt it was sad that there was no-one to admire her except the birds and the bees.

She thought, whatever Oliver Mell had said to her in flattering tones, that his eyes had been critical.

She knew that, like Lady Isabel, he resented her presence.

As she walked towards the Study, she hoped he was not upsetting the Marquis.

She was longing to know if her treatment last night had made him feel better and his eyes stronger.

She reached the Study door and heard Oliver Mell saying:

"I have written out the cheque, Michael."

"Cranley will do that for you," the Marquis replied.

"I would rather he did not know of what is really a private transaction between us," Oliver Mell said in a lofty tone. "Servants talk. All you have to do is to sign it."

"Oh, very well," the Marquis said. "Bring me some ink and a pen."

Erlina walked into the room.

She saw that the Marquis was sitting in an armchair.

Oliver Mell had already reached the writing-desk which stood in the window.

"Is that you, Erlina?" the Marquis asked. "I was told you had gone riding. Did you enjoy yourself?"

"Yes, thank you very much," Erlina replied. "I rode the horse I like best, which is *Juno*."

"I approve your choice," the Marquis remarked.

Oliver Mell was searching among the things on the desk.

"There is ink here," he said, "but I cannot find a quill."

"I think I know where the new ones are," Erlina offered.

She walked to the desk, opened a drawer, and

took out a new long white quill pen.

She went towards the Marquis with it.

Oliver Mell followed her with the ink-pot in one hand and the cheque he had made out for the Marquis to sign in the other.

Erlina noticed that the Marquis had taken a book from the table beside him and laid it on his knees.

In that way she knew he could sign the cheque more easily.

Oliver put the cheque down in front of the Marquis, keeping his hand on it as if he thought it might slip.

He looked enquiringly at Erlina.

It suddenly struck her that he was carefully hiding from her the amount that was written on the cheque.

On an impulse she dropped the quill pen onto the floor.

There was nothing Oliver Mell could do but bend down and pick it up.

As he did so, Erlina looked at the cheque.

Then she gave a little cry.

"You have made a mistake!" she said. "You have put one nought too many! His Lordship said he would pay one thousand pounds for *Titus,* not ten thousand!"

She saw the fury in Oliver Mell's face before the Marquis said:

"Up to your tricks again, Oliver! I might have guessed why you were in such a hurry for me to sign the money over to you."

"It was a mistake—of course it was a mistake!"

Oliver Mell said sharply. "I will write out another cheque."

He picked up the one in front of the Marquis and walked back to the desk.

"Do not waste your time," the Marquis said sarcastically. "I will have Cranley do it instead. I would prefer him to help me sign it, rather than you."

Oliver Mell did not reply.

He merely walked across the room, opened the door, and went out slamming it behind him.

The Marquis sighed.

"I might have known he would try to cheat me!" he said.

"He behaved absolutely disgracefully," Erlina said, "and I shall be glad when he has gone tomorrow."

"So shall I," the Marquis admitted. "I never thought he would find me here."

"You do not think when they go back to London they will tell your friends where you are?" Erlina asked. "Crowds of people may come rushing down to see you!"

"I can only hope that will not happen," the Marquis answered. "If they do, you will have to hide me."

"That might be difficult," Erlina said. "Are there any secret passages, or Priest's holes in the Hall?"

"If there are, I have never found them," the Marquis replied.

"Then we will have to think of some other hiding-place," Erlina said. "In the meantime, if your eyes get better, perhaps you will want to go back to London."

"Is that what you want me to do?" the Marquis asked.

"No, of course not! You know I want you to stay here with Gerry and me. When your friends arrive they seem . . . to . . . spoil . . . everything."

There was a little sob in her voice, which the Marquis did not miss.

Then he said quietly:

"We think the same on a great many subjects, Erlina. I would like you now to play for me again."

Erlina smiled at him.

"I would love to do that," she answered, "if you will just allow me five minutes in which to eat my breakfast."

"You have not eaten?" the Marquis asked. "I thought, of course, you would have had breakfast before you went riding."

"I was in too much of a hurry to get to the stables," Erlina answered. "But I promise I will not keep you waiting more than five minutes, and I will get Hignet to take you to the Music Room."

She jumped up, and hurried out of the Study.

She reached the Breakfast-Room to find the boys eating the delicious dishes which Mrs. Dawes had prepared.

It was so different from the one egg, which was the most Gerry had been able to have in the old days at Sherwood House.

Sometimes there was nothing but toast with a scraping of butter.

For Tom things had been very much the same, and after he finished everything on his plate he said in a heartfelt tone:

"I hope His Lordship stays here for ever and ever! Then we can ride his horses and eat his scrumptious food!"

"That is what I say too!" Gerry chimed in.

Erlina agreed with them.

She had been afraid, when his Cousin and Lady Isabel arrived, the Marquis would not want them in the house.

Or, he might have decided to go back to London.

She felt she must keep her fingers crossed and pray that he would still want her services as he needed them now.

She ate very quickly and, having told the boys what they were to do, ran to the Music Room.

The Marquis was sitting at the open window where he had been yesterday.

Without speaking, she went to the piano.

She sat down and started to play what came into her mind first.

There was joy in her music because he had let her try to heal his eyes, and because he liked her playing to him.

She went on to tell him through her playing how happy she was that he was putting right everything that had gone wrong.

She was pleased that people were returning to the village, and men were working on the land, and in the garden.

The music went on to tell him that the house

was looking clean and beautiful, as it had been in the past.

She poured it all out.

Only when she had played for a long time did she think that perhaps the Marquis might be getting bored.

She took her hands from the keys and put them in her lap.

For what seemed a long time he did not speak.

Then he said quietly:

"Thank you, Erlina! That is just what I want you to feel."

"You . . . understood what I . . . was saying?" she asked.

"I think by now you realise that I not only understand, but I feel the same way," he answered.

She made a little murmur of delight.

Then she walked to his chair and, without asking, bent over to put her hands over his eyes.

It was not quite the same as when last night she had been able to try to heal him without the bandage.

Still, as she prayed, she felt uplifted.

She knew that he was seeing the light which would heal him.

* * *

It was luncheon time before Lady Isabel appeared.

Erlina was glad that everybody was assembled in the Drawing-Room and she was not alone.

She was quiet during the meal while Lady Isabel was determined to monopolize the Marquis.

Oliver Mell was sulky because he had been exposed over the cheque.

After he left the Music Room, the Marquis had given Mr. Cranley orders to write out a cheque for one thousand pounds.

When he had signed it, he told him to give it to his Cousin.

Erlina knew by the expression on Mr. Cranley's face that he disapproved of the transaction.

It was not his business, however, to comment on it.

In fact, he brought good news.

He had found another firm of builders who were prepared to start work in the village immediately.

He also had two housemaids and another footman moving into the Hall the next day.

"They are all young, My Lord, and prepared to work hard," Mr. Cranley told the Marquis, "and I hope to find a Housekeeper next time I go to Boxstead."

"I doubt if anyone could run the house better than Miss Sherwood," the Marquis said, "and we need a lot more staff to get the place clean. I can only beg you, Cranley, to go on collecting them."

"I am doing my best, My Lord," Mr. Cranley replied.

There was another Farmer coming after luncheon to talk to the Marquis about renting one of the outlying farms.

The Marquis had arranged to see him in the Study.

Erlina was for the moment alone in the Drawing-Room.

She was just thinking there was quite a lot of cleaning still to be done, when Gerry came running into the room.

"Tom has had to go home," he said. "His Mother wants him this afternoon."

"What are you going to do?" Erlina asked.

"I am going to look at the secret the Marquis told me about."

"That will keep you busy," she said.

Gerry hurried away.

Erlina sat down to look at a book which she had noticed in the Library.

It was about an explorer who had visited India and reached the foothills of the Himalayas.

There was a long description of the people he had met, many of them being Gurus, Sooth-Sayers, and, of course, Healers.

He described how successful the Healers were.

What particularly interested Erlina was how they worked to heal the sight of children as well as old people.

She was deep in the book, when Gerry came bursting into the room.

"Come with me, Erlina!" he begged. "Come with me at once! I have something really exciting to show you!"

"What is it?" Erlina asked, putting down the book reluctantly.

"It is the secret His Lordship told me, and he said, if I wanted to, I could tell you."

"Did he really?" Erlina aksed.

Gerry nodded.

Then he put his hand out, and pulled her towards the door.

"Come on, come on," he said. "It is very exciting!"

They went out into the garden.

Walking over the still-unkempt lawn, they passed through a clump of rhododendron bushes.

Gerry climbed ahead up a twisting path, until they came to what Erlina saw was a Summer House.

It was a very attractive one, although the paint on the windows had peeled away.

When she looked inside she saw there were leaves on the floor, which had blown in during the Autumn.

There was a wooden seat on which the cushions were faded and torn with age.

"Is this what you have found?" she asked.

"Come—come with me!" Gerry persisted.

He took her round to the back of the summer house, and she wondered what the secret was.

Then Gerry started to climb up the side of it.

Erlina saw there were iron footholds on what must have been the trunk of a tree.

"Follow me, follow me!" Gerry cried excitedly.

Because Erlina understood now what this was all about, she climbed up after him.

On the top of the Summer House there was an aperture which was not noticeable from the front.

It opened into the space inside between the floor boards, and the top of the roof which was pointed.

It was this hiding-place the Marquis had

described to Gerry, which as a boy he had obviously used himself.

There were a number of things in it which he must have kept there.

They had remained undiscovered after he had grown up.

There were horse-shoes he had collected in the stables, and rough carvings he might have done himself.

There were several whistles, a huntsman's horn, and a riding-crop.

Some very tattered books looked as if they had been nibbled by mice.

It was a perfect hiding-place for a small boy who wanted to escape from his Nurse or his Tutors.

"His Lordship told me that he used to hide here," Gerry was saying, "and although they called and called, no-one ever found where he was hiding."

Erlina sat down on the floor.

Gerry could stand up, although he had to bend his head except in the centre of the floor.

Erlina was too tall to do anything but sit.

"I think it is a very nice place for you to have all to yourself," she said, "and tomorrow I will clean it out for you."

"I thought that was what you would say," Gerry replied. "I'll help you, and will bring up my bow and arrows and some of the other things I found in the attic."

"That is a good idea," Erlina agreed.

She thought it important for him to have a place which he could call his own.

Gerry was thinking it out.

"I will ask Mrs. Dawes," he said, "if she will give me a tin of biscuits which I can eat up here when I am hungry."

"I am sure she will," Erlina said, "and as the rug on the floor is rather dirty, we might find a new one and also some cushions on which to sit."

"That is a spiffing idea!" Gerry approved.

When Erlina pulled back the rug from the floor as she spoke, she realised that the boards beneath it had shrunk a little over the years.

It was easy, therefore, to look down into the Summer House itself.

It was, however, quite safe as the boards rested on heavy beams which were, she felt, indestructible.

She was thinking there were plenty of things in the house which she and Gerry could bring out here.

Suddenly she heard someone speak below.

She looked down through the crack between the boards.

To her surprise, she saw that it was Oliver Mell and Lady Isabel who were standing below them.

Gerry saw them too, and Erlina put her finger to her lips to warn him not to speak.

Then she knew it was unnecessary because he would certainly not want them to be aware of his secret hiding-place.

In fact, he sat down on the floor, taking care not to make a noise with his feet.

"I brought you here," Oliver Mell was saying, "because I have to talk to you, and I am always afraid Michael's accursed servants are listening at the doors."

"You are quite right," Lady Isabel agreed, "and that Valet of his is always creeping about."

"I told you that damned girl prevented me from getting a little money out of Michael," Oliver Mell said. "It was just like her to walk through the door at the most awkward moment."

"She would do that," Lady Isabel said spitefully, "and the sooner we get rid of her, the better!"

"What we have to do first," Oliver Mell reminded her, "is to get rid of Michael."

"I know that," Lady Isabel said, "but you were not very successful the first time you tried it."

"Anybody else," Oliver Mell fumed, "who would have fallen from his horse when the branch struck him across the face would have been kicked by the animal, and ended up by being killed!"

"But none of those things happened," Lady Isabel replied, "and what is more, Michael believes he will soon be able to see again."

"That is something that has to be prevented," Oliver Mell said. "You do realise, Isabel, that unless I can settle my debts, I will end up in prison?"

Lady Isabel gave a little cry.

"Oh, Darling, that cannot happen!"

"I know, I know," he said, "and it is only Michael who stands between me and an enormous fortune. He is as rich as Croesus!"

The greedy note in his voice was very unpleasant.

"He is also preventing you from being the Marquis of Meldon," Lady Isabel said softly.

"That is true," Oliver Mell said testily. "That is why we have to get rid of him before we leave tomorrow morning."

"I wonder what excuse we could make for staying on?" Lady Isabel murmured.

"My excuse will be that I have to attend my Cousin's Funeral," Oliver Mell retorted.

"But how? How?" Lady Isabel asked.

Oliver Mell put his arm around her and pulled her down onto the wooden seat.

"Now listen to what I have planned," he said, "and once we leave the Summer House, we must not speak of it again."

"I am listening," Lady Isabel said eagerly.

"I have brought with me a very strong poison," Oliver Mell said, "which when put into a man's wine makes him appear to be very drunk."

"You will give it to him at dinner?" Lady Isabel asked.

"That is my intention," Oliver Mell said. "Then Michael will appear drunk, very, very drunk, so much so that he will have to be helped, if not carried upstairs to bed."

Lady Isabel drew in her breath.

"What then?" she asked.

"As I have told you before, his bedroom has a special window which was put in by Michael's grandfather. It would be very easy for a man, especially if he was drunk, to fall out of it. And that is what Michael will do."

He spoke quietly, but there was a note of elation in his voice.

He was relishing the idea of his Cousin's death.

"It sounds all right," Lady Isabel said slowly.

"It is foolproof," Oliver Mell assured her. "Do you not see? No-one can connect me with it. Michael gets drunk at dinner and because he is blind falls out of the window."

He looked at her to see if she understood before he went on:

"He will break his neck when he falls onto the terrace from that window, and nobody can possibly be blamed for a mistake made by a blind man."

"You are really very clever, Darling," Lady Isabel said in her cooing voice. "I shall enjoy being the Marchioness of Meldon and having unlimited money to spend in London."

"Just as I shall enjoy being the Marquis, after being pushed off with a mere pittance to call my own!" Oliver Mell said fervently.

"All that will be changed after to-morrow," Lady Isabel said fervently. "And do not let there be any mistakes. After all, you were certain he would be killed in that Steeple-Chase."

"Instead of which poor old Philip died," Oliver Mell murmured.

"There is nothing you can do about that now," Lady Isabel remarked, "and I think we ought to be going back."

"I had to tell you what I was doing," Oliver Mell said. "You must go on appearing loving and concerned about him to impress the servants."

"I thought I was doing that rather well," Lady Isabel answered.

"You are brilliant, you know that!" Oliver Mell assured her. "And when I am not so harassed as I am now, I will be able to tell you just how much you mean to me."

He pulled her closer and kissed her passionately.

Erlina shut her eyes.

She could hardly believe what she had heard!

How could anything so wicked and appalling have been planned by one man against another?

Oliver released Lady Isabel.

"Come along, my Darling," he said. "Back to work! There will be time to relax, and for me to tell you how much you excite me when all this is over."

"Oh, Oliver, I want you now!" Lady Isabel protested.

"It would be a mistake to linger," he replied. "Who knows, one of those accursed servants may be looking for us, or Michael may be asking for you."

"I doubt it, so long as he has got that idiotic girl with him!" Lady Isabel said viciously. "The first thing you must do as soon as he is dead is to push her and that brat out of the house!"

"I will do so with relish!" Oliver said. "I will never forgive her for stopping Michael from signing that cheque!"

They were walking away as he spoke. Erlina did not hear Lady Isabel's reply.

For a moment it was difficult to realise that what she had heard was real and not a figment of her imagination.

How could any two people who were well-born

plan in such a cold-blooded manner anything so horrible as the Marquis's death?

Then she realised that sitting beside her Gerry was looking pale and frightened.

"Did you ... hear what ... they were ... saying?" he asked in a whisper.

Erlina put her arm round him.

"Yes, I heard," she answered, "and they are wicked, wicked people. We have got to stop them from killing the Marquis, who has been so kind to us."

"How can ... we do ... that?" Gerry asked.

Because she was thinking, Erlina did not reply and he went on:

"If you prevent them from ... killing him ... tonight, they will ... try again. They want his ... money and because he is ... blind he will not be able to ... stop them from getting it."

Erlina held her brother close.

"It was incredibly lucky," she said, "that you and I were here and learned of their wicked plans. Now we have to be clever."

"In what ... way?" Gerry asked.

"First of all," Erlina said, "they must never for a moment suspect that we overheard what they were planning. We must, therefore, behave perfectly normally just as we have done up until now."

"That is ... going to be very difficult," Gerry replied. "I would like to shoot them with my bow and arrows. I wish I was old enough to use a gun."

"Then we would be criminals," Erlina said. "We

must not do anything wrong, and certainly we must not kill anyone."

"Then how will we stop them from . . . killing . . . the Marquis?" Gerry asked again.

Erlina knew as she held him close that he was frightened.

She thought it was not surprising, for she too felt desperately afraid of Oliver Mell.

She was quite certain he would not hesitate to dispose of them both if he learned that they knew his secret.

But how could she allow anyone so despicable, so evil, to kill a man like the Marquis?

Even as she asked herself the question, she remembered how she herself had hated the Marquis in the first place. She had actually hoped that he would die miserably.

Now she knew she would do anything rather than let him lose his life.

Quite suddenly, like a flash of lightning, she knew that she loved him.

She could hardly believe that was true.

Yet as she walked back hand-in-hand with Gerry, keeping to the shrubs, she knew she would rather die herself than have him suffer any more.

Now that she had learnt that Oliver Mell had deliberately planned his destruction during the Steeple-Chase, she had to do something to stop him.

Because he was Heir Presumptive and would take his Cousin's place, he would never rest until the Marquis was dead.

"What can . . . I do? What . . . can I . . . do?" she asked herself frantically.

She knew by the way Gerry was holding on to her hand that he was afraid she would not find an answer.

They reached the house.

Instead of going in by the front-door, they entered by one of the garden doors.

In this way Erlina hoped to avoid any confrontation with Oliver Mell or Lady Isabel.

They went up a side staircase to Gerry's bedroom.

When they were inside, Gerry put his arms round Erlina's neck, and hid his face against her shoulder.

"I am . . . frightened, Erlina!" he said. "Frightened that they will . . . kill the . . . Marquis! And you . . . heard what . . . they said they . . . would do to . . . us!"

Erlina drew her brother down so that they both sat on the bed.

"Now, listen, Gerry," she said, "we have to be very calm and not in any way make Oliver Mell suspicious that we are watching him, or make him feel that anything has changed since yesterday."

She knew Gerry was listening and she said:

"I want you to stay here in your room while I go down and see if I can talk to the Marquis."

"Will you tell him?" Gerry asked.

"I have got to prevent him from drinking the poison that Oliver Mell intends to put into his wine tonight."

She paused and then went on:

"But it would be a mistake for him to get so

angry that he accuses his Cousin of trying to murder him."

She thought for a moment. Then she said:

"You were right when you said that if they fail again this time, they will go on trying. We have to do something to prevent Oliver Mell from coming anywhere near His Lordship from now on."

Erlina was trying to sort things out in her mind.

Then she asked:

"Would you be happier if you went to the Vicarage and asked if you could stay the night with Tom? I am sure they would be pleased to have you."

Gerry looked at his sister.

She knew he was turning the question over in his mind.

Then, as if he suddenly became grown up, he said:

"I think, Erlina, I ought to stay with you. After all, I am a man and I have to look after you."

As she bent forward to kiss his cheek, Erlina felt tears come into her eyes.

"That is very brave of you," she told him, "and I know it is exactly what Papa would have said."

"Papa would have said that I must fight for what is right and good," Gerry remarked, "and Mr. Mell is a bad and wicked man."

"Then we will fight him together!" Erlina declared.

She wiped her tears away, and kissed Gerry again.

"Now, you stay here," she said, "while I go to find out what is happening. Will you be all right?"

"I think I will go up to the attic," Gerry said, "and bring down one of those duelling pistols."

Erlina thought it was a good idea and could do no harm.

"All right," she said, "and look and see if there is anything else you want to take up to your secret hiding-place."

As she spoke she hoped that it would remain a secret place for a long time.

They went out of the bedroom together.

Erlina went along the corridor towards the stairs.

Gerry walked in the opposite direction towards the North Wing.

Slowly, because she was frightened, Erlina went down the stairs.

Dawes was in the hall, instructing a new footman how he should behave when he was on duty.

She passed them by without speaking, and walked towards the Study.

Just before she reached the door, Mr. Cranley came out.

With him was a tall, strong-looking man whom she guessed must be the farmer who had come to be interviewed by the Marquis.

"Good afternoon, Miss Sherwood," Mr. Cranley said.

"Good afternoon, Mr. Cranley," Erlina replied. "Is His Lordship alone?"

"Yes, we have finished our interview, and it has been most satisfactory," Mr. Cranley replied.

"I am so glad." Erlina smiled.

She opened the Study door, and saw the

Marquis sitting in his favourite armchair.

For a moment she forgot everything except that he looked so handsome, so strong, and so very attractive.

There was only the black bandage over his eyes to spoil the picture.

She wanted more than anything to run across to him, and tell him how much he meant to her.

Then she remembered that she meant very little to him.

She was useful in helping him with the house.

He also believed that in some miraculous way she could cure his blindness.

If she did so, he would be extremely grateful.

She could not remember his showing her in any way that he thought of her as an attractive woman.

Or, indeed, as a woman at all.

He had been concerned only with what she could do to help him.

He had worried about how his friends would see him.

But she was not important enough for him to worry about how he appeared to her as a blind man.

It all passed swiftly through her mind.

If she showed the Marquis she was one of what Hignet had called the 'bees round a honey-pot' he might easily despise her.

"Them never lasts long!" Hignet had said.

Erlina must have stood just inside the door for a few seconds.

Yet, it seemed to her that a century of thoughts had passed through her mind.

Now she felt as if there were a stone in her breast, instead of her heart.

"Is that you, Erlina?" the Marquis asked.

"Yes," she answered. "I gather your interview was a great success."

"The Farmer is a nice man. I am sure he will do well. I have let him the farm at quite a reasonable rent."

"I am so glad," Erlina said. "Now we shall no longer see all those fields going to waste."

She spoke without thinking.

"*See* them going to waste?" the Marquis repeated. "That is the operative word, is it not, Erlina? Will I see them, or will you just have to tell me about them?"

"You *will* see them!" Erlina said. "I promise you that."

It was more of a vow than a promise.

She told herself that she would kill Oliver Mell herself before she'd break this promise to the Marquis.

chapter seven

ERLINA went closer to the Marquis.

In a voice he could hardly hear she said:

"Will you . . . come into . . . the Music Room? I have . . . something to . . . tell you."

The Marquis raised his eye-brows.

"The Music Room?" he questioned reflectively.

Erlina did not answer.

She merely waited. He rose to his feet.

He put his hand on her shoulder in the same way as he did when Gerry guided him.

It was the first time he had done so.

Erlina felt a thrill because he was touching her.

With difficulty, she managed to concentrate on getting him through the door, and down the passage.

The Music Room was at the end of it.

She felt she could safely talk to him there without anyone overhearing their conversation.

She was thinking of what she had heard.

She saw to her relief that the Marquis's chair had been moved back from the window to the middle of the room.

She felt sure that nothing she said would be overheard.

The Marquis seated himself, crossed his legs, and asked:

"Now then, what is all this about? I can tell you are upset."

"Very . . . upset," Erlina replied.

She went down on her knees beside him, then said:

"I have . . . something very . . . important to . . . tell you. You are in great danger!"

"That does not surprise me," the Marquis replied, "but if I am, how have you found out about it?"

Bending forward so that her face was only a little way from his, Erlina began to whisper.

She told him exactly what she and Gerry had overheard from the secret hiding-place on top of the Summer House.

It took a little time because she stumbled over the words.

It was difficult to keep the horror out of her voice as she spoke.

She told the Marquis how she and Gerry had walked back to the house through the shrubs so that they would not be seen.

"What . . . can you . . . do? What can . . . you do?" she asked finally. "As Gerry said . . . if your Cousin fails . . . this time . . . he will . . . try again."

The Marquis put out his hand and found hers.

He was aware that Erlina was trembling.

Then he said:

"The only thing that matters is that you have warned me. Now I have to think out how I can prevent Oliver not only from killing me this time, but from trying again."

"This will be his . . . second . . . attempt," Erlina said miserably. "It was he who was . . . responsible for your . . . damaging your . . . eyes."

"I rather suspected that," the Marquis said, "and I was a fool to agree to the Steeple-Chase in the first place!"

"But now that . . . you know how wicked he is," Erlina persisted, "you must . . . save yourself. How can you . . . die in such a . . . meaningless manner?"

"I agree with you," the Marquis said. "It would be most humiliating to be killed by my disreputable Cousin because he wants my money."

"And your . . . title," Erlina added.

"It never struck me for a moment," the Marquis went on, "that Isabel would transfer her affections from me to Oliver. She obviously thinks he would be easier to manipulate than she found I was."

"It is . . . all so evil and . . . wicked that I cannot . . . believe it is true," Erlina said miserably.

"You should not be mixed up in this sort of degrading situation," the Marquis said sharply.

"But I am ... mixed up ... in it," Erlina retorted, "and Gerry and I ... have to ... help you ... we have ... to!"

The Marquis's hands held hers even more firmly.

"I do not intend to let Oliver win," he said.

"But ... how can you ... prevent it?" Erlina asked. "And even if you do ... not drink the ... wine, he may still ... try to push you ... out of the ... window."

She paused before she added:

"He said ... something about the window having been specially put ... there by your ... grandfather. What did he ... mean?"

"I had forgotten that you had been in my bedroom only in the dark," the Marquis answered. "The room had three large Georgian sash windows, like those in the rest of the house, which, as you know, lift up from the bottom or come down from the top. They can only be half-opened at any one time."

Erlina was listening, and he went on;

"My Grandfather suffered from high blood-pressure and was always feeling he could not breathe properly. He, therefore, had one of the Georgian windows removed and replaced by a large casement which opens outwards."

He stopped for a moment and then continued:

"As all the windows have very low sills, it can be quite dangerous, and in Oliver's mind a very convenient way of getting rid of me."

Erlina gave a little cry.

"You must not ... go near the ... window! You

must have it . . . barred or . . . boarded up."

"There is no time to do that before tonight," the Marquis replied, "and anyway, as you yourself have said, he will go on trying in one way or another until he succeeds in murdering me."

"I . . . I cannot . . . bear it," Erlina cried. "Stop him . . . you have to . . . stop him!"

The Marquis was silent for a moment.

Then he said:

"Does it mean so much to you?"

She was aware that she had betrayed her feelings.

Because she did not want him to know the truth, she said quietly:

"How could I . . . not be . . . upset and . . . appalled at this . . . happening to anyone and especially to . . . you when you . . . have been so . . . kind to Gerry and . . . me."

"I understand," the Marquis said in a different tone. "And if I die, Oliver will certainly turn you out the very next day."

"We have . . . nowhere . . . to go," Erlina murmured.

"I realise that," the Marquis replied.

He was aware as she spoke that she was still trembling, and he said quietly:

"Now go and play for me on the piano while I plan how I can outwit my outrageous Cousin. Perhaps the answer will come to me in your music, or from the light you bring me from Heaven."

"It will . . . I am sure . . . it will," Erlina said.

She took her hand away from his, and rose to her feet.

For a second she stood looking down at him, wishing she could tell him how much she loved him.

Then, afraid of her own thoughts, she went to the piano.

She started to play the music of the woods, the flowers, the birds, and the bees as she had before.

Yet somehow her heart took over and, without really meaning to, she poured out her love.

She felt that in some way it must help him and save him.

She played for a long time, until she wondered if the Marquis had gone to sleep.

Finally he said:

"Thank you, Erlina."

She took her hands from the keys and he went on:

"I have it all worked out, and now I want you to take me upstairs to my bedroom."

While he was speaking, Erlina had moved from the piano to stand beside his chair.

"Are you . . . wise to go . . . there?" she asked.

"I am quite safe until Oliver gives me the wine that is poisoned," the Marquis answered, "and I want to talk to Hignet."

He got up from his chair and put his hand on her shoulder as he had done before.

They walked from the Music Room along the passage to the hall.

Hignet was there, speaking to Dawes, and when he saw the Marquis, he exclaimed:

"Oh, there you are, M'Lord. I was comin' t'tell you that the postman's been an' there's some letters which I've put on your desk. Mr. Cranley ain't in t'house."

"They can wait," the Marquis said. "I want you now, Hignet, to take me to my bedroom."

He took his hand from Erlina's shoulder as he spoke.

She felt as he went up the stairs as if he were going away from her, and she might never be near him again.

"Tea'll be ready in a few minutes in th' Drawing-Room, Miss," Dawes said. " 'Er Ladyship wants it early."

"Then bring it as quickly as you can," Erlina replied.

She knew she must force herself to behave quite naturally.

She thought, perhaps, it would be a mistake to send for Gerry.

Even the way he looked at them might make Oliver Mell and Lady Isabel suspicious.

Therefore when tea arrived, she poured out as she always did.

Then she arranged an assortment of cakes and sandwiches on a plate.

As she did so, she murmured something about Gerry playing upstairs, but Oliver Mell and Lady Isabel were obviously not interested.

It was a relief to escape from them, and go upstairs to Gerry's bedroom.

He had brought down two duelling-pistols from the attic and was cleaning them on his bed.

"I could not find any bullets, Erlina," he said despondently.

"You are not to think of shooting with those

141

pistols," she admonished him.

"I thought I could protect the Marquis with them."

"We are going to protect the Marquis by doing exactly what he tells us to do."

"You have told him what they mean to do?" Gerry asked.

"I have, and he knows that he has to save himself."

"You warned him that the wine would be poisoned?"

Erlina put her finger up to her lips.

"Not so loud!" she said, "it is a mistake even to talk about it. The Marquis knows everything, and he has a plan which I am sure he will tell us about in due course."

"He will have to be very careful," Gerry said warningly.

"I know that," Erlina agreed.

There was no message from the Marquis before they went to dress for dinner.

Only after Erlina had finished dressing and was ready to go downstairs was there a knock on the door.

She opened it and Hignet came into the room.

He shut the door behind him and said in a low voice, afraid of being overheard:

" 'Is Lordship's got everythin' planned, Miss. You an' Sir Gerald are to behave quite normal-like an' not look worried."

"That is easier said than done," Erlina murmured.

"I knows, Miss," Hignet said, "but we'll defeat

those devils, one way or 'nother, so don't you worry!"

"Are you . . . sure His Lordship will be . . . all right?" Erlina asked in a whisper.

"He's too clever t' be done in by a pusher like Mr. Oliver!" Hignet said. "He's told me t' tell you that when 'e leaves the Dining-Room pretending t' have drunk too much, you an' Sir Gerald is t' follow us up th' stairs to 'is bedroom."

Erlina looked surprised.

Before, however, she could ask any questions, Hignet had opened the door and slipped out.

She knew he did not want to be seen by Oliver Mell or Lady Isabel.

They were late coming downstairs.

Erlina and Gerry found the Marquis alone in the Drawing-Room.

He appeared to be completely at his ease and in no way perturbed.

As soon as they joined him, he started to talk about the Farmer to whom he had let a farm.

He told them what crops he had planned with him to plant.

"We have to be clever," he said, "and that includes you, Gerry, with your land. We must grow crops which are not being undercut by cheap imports from abroad, but which are indispensable to this country."

"I do not suppose anyone will want to farm my land," Gerry said.

"I am going to farm it for you," the Marquis answered. "But you have to work with me in taking an interest in what is happening, and you must learn all about the rotation of crops and

143

a great many other things so that you will not make any mistakes when you do all the farming yourself."

"That will be fun," Gerry exclaimed.

Lady Isabel and Oliver Mell, who had entered while the Marquis was talking, heard the end of the conversation.

"I am sure, Michael," he said, "that you are giving Gerry very good advice, and this Estate certainly wants a great deal done to it!"

"I know," the Marquis agreed, "and I am already planning how I can bring in new ideas and of course more labourers."

He was still talking about farming as they walked towards the Dining-Room.

It was obvious to Erlina that the subject bored Oliver Mell.

She thought it was clever of the Marquis, however, to pick a subject which involved the future.

She was sure this would convince his Cousin that he had no suspicion of what might happen to him in the immediate present.

Lady Isabel was determined to turn the conversation round to herself.

She began in her usual manner to flirt with the Marquis, ignoring everybody else at the table.

"And what have you been doing with your beautiful self?" Oliver Mell asked Erlina.

"I have been practising on the piano, for one thing," she answered, "and enjoying the sunshine, for another."

"You have not been over to see your house?" he asked.

144

She thought he was trying to make her upset about it, and she replied:

"There is nothing I can do at the moment, so I try not to think about it."

"How long do you intend to be a guest at Meldon Hall?" he asked.

"For as long as the Marquis will have us," Erlina replied lightly. "I feel sure I am really helping his eyes and that he will soon be able to see again."

She saw a mocking twist at the corners of Oliver Mell's mouth.

She thought how utterly and completely despicable he was.

Then, afraid he might see in her eyes what she was thinking, she started to talk about horses.

She told him how much she enjoyed riding the Marquis's.

"I meant to go riding today," Oliver Mell said in a lofty tone, "but I will make up for it tomorrow, and perhaps you will accompany me?"

"That would be delightful," Erlina replied.

She hoped she would be forgiven for lying.

It was with an effort that she kept the conversation going while Lady Isabel monopolised the Marquis.

At last the excellent dinner that Mrs. Dawes had cooked came to an end.

It was then that Oliver Mell said:

"I have a surprise for you, Michael."

"What is it?" the Marquis asked.

"Before I left London, His Royal Highness gave me a present to bring you which I know you will enjoy and appreciate."

"A present?" the Marquis exclaimed.

"I did not produce it yesterday," Oliver Mell went on, "in order to give it time to settle, but I have given it to Dawes to uncork and decant, and it is something very special."

"What is it?" the Marquis enquired again.

"It is a bottle of very fine Tawny Port, which the Prince Regent told me has been kept in wood for over fifteen years."

"That certainly sounds interesting," the Marquis remarked.

"It is not only interesting," Oliver Mell said, "but owing to the war, as you know, there is not much well matured Port in England. The members of White's Club have drunk it all up!"

It was then that Dawes appeared with a decanter in his hands.

He put it down on the table in front of the Marquis.

"I am deeply obliged to His Royal Highness," the Marquis said, "and I hope, Oliver, that you will join me."

"The Prince Regent made it very clear that the present was for you, not for me," Oliver said.

He made it sound as if he rather resented the fact, in what Erlina thought was a very convincing manner.

"As it happens," he went on, "I find Port too heavy for my taste, and I prefer this excellent claret you have provided. But please allow me to pour some Port into your glass."

"I do not like to drink alone," the Marquis said as he did so, "and it is sad if nobody else will join me. Perhaps you will take a glass, Isabel?"

Lady Isabel screwed up her nose.

"I prefer champagne," she said.

The Marquis gave a sigh and picked up his glass.

"I wonder if you know, Erlina," Oliver asked, "that Port comes from Portugal?"

"My Father told me that it comes from Oporto," Erlina replied, "and that it was actually invented by the English when, thanks to the Methuen Treaties, the wines of Portugal were the only wines available to them."

"Goodness me! You are well informed!" Oliver exclaimed.

"I hope so," Erlina replied, "and in case you had forgotten, the Methuen Treaties were signed in 1703."

"You have certainly impressed me with your knowledge!" Oliver said in an affected tone of voice.

"I, too, am impressed," the Marquis agreed, "and I find this Port delicious. You are quite sure, Oliver, you will not have a glass?"

"I would not deprive you of what is a unique present," Oliver Mell replied, "and to please His Royal Highness, you must drink it all yourself."

"But not at one sitting!" the Marquis protested. "The decanter can remain here and I will have a glass or two every night."

Watching Oliver, Erlina knew he was thinking that there would not be another night for the Marquis.

With an effort, she made herself look away and talk to Gerry.

He had hardly spoken a word all through dinner.

She had warned him before they came downstairs to be very careful.

She felt proud of the small boy who was carrying out her instructions perfectly.

She was quite certain Oliver had never given him a second glance.

The Marquis finished his glass of Port.

Now there was a silence round the table, as both Oliver Mell and Lady Isabel looked at him.

It was then he said: "Hignet!" in a slurred tone.

Hignet, who was standing by the sideboard with Dawes, hurried to his side.

"I do not—feel very—well," the Marquis said thickly. "Get me—up-upstairs—and—q-quickly!"

Hignet helped him out of his chair.

It was obvious as they walked towards the door, that the Marquis was stumbling and having difficulty in putting one foot in front of the other.

Only as the door closed behind them did Erlina say:

"What is wrong? What can have upset him? He seemed so well when he sat down to dinner."

"I think perhaps he has had too much to drink," Oliver Mell suggested in a soothing voice. "Port can be very heady, especially when one has been drinking champagne and claret."

"I think I should go to see that he has everything he needs," Erlina said, rising to her feet.

"I am sure Hignet can manage," Oliver Mell

interposed, "and he will soon sleep it off."

Erlina did not reply.

She merely turned towards the door. Gerry followed her.

She thought as she left the room that Oliver Mell and Lady Isabel would be exchanging glances of satisfaction at what had occurred.

Away from the Dining-Room, she and Gerry ran across the hall, and up the stairs.

They went, as the Marquis had told them to, to his bedroom.

When they entered, Erlina saw that Hignet was pulling the curtains over the windows and shutting out the sunshine.

The Marquis, looking exactly like his usual self, said as he heard them come in:

"There is no hurry. Oliver will not come until he thinks Hignet has got me to bed and left me alone."

"You were very clever the way you walked in that funny way to the door!" Gerry said admiringly. "Mr. Mell thought you had had too much to drink."

"That is what I was hoping he would think," the Marquis answered. "Now, we must talk very quietly, or not at all. Hignet will shortly go downstairs to tell my Cousin that I am safely in bed. In the meantime we have to be ready."

"What are you . . . going to . . . do?" Erlina asked nervously.

She was looking, as she spoke, at the window which the Marquis had described to her.

She could see it was different from the other two.

149

Hignet was closing the casement, and pulling the curtains over it.

There were three candles beside the bed, illuminating the room.

The Marquis took Erlina by the hand and asked her to guide him to a corner of the room beyond the windows.

There was an attractive screen, and behind it Erlina saw there were two chairs and a stool.

"This is where we are going to sit," he said in a low voice, "while the drama takes place."

Erlina did not understand, but did not ask any questions.

She only sat down on one of the chairs and Gerry sat on the stool.

As she did so, she said to the Marquis in a soft voice:

"You do not think it is a mistake for Gerry to be here?"

"I want him as a witness," the Marquis answered. "It would be a mistake for you to be the only person who had seen what Oliver was planning to do."

The word 'witness' made Erlina shudder.

If what was happening was brought to Court, she could imagine what a scandal it would be.

She realised how horrified the Marquis's friends and relatives would be.

She knew she must not ask questions, however.

She only sat quietly on the chair, with Gerry on the stool beside her.

The Marquis went across the room, and had a whispered conversation with Hignet.

The Valet brought him back, and then left the room.

"I am afraid we are going to have a long wait," the Marquis said, "but at least we are all together."

Erlina thought it was a touching thing to say, and it was what she felt herself.

She could not help being terrified in case this was the last time they would be together.

However cleverly the Marquis tried to prevent it, Oliver Mell would continue trying to find a way of murdering him.

It was about five minutes later that Hignet returned.

He did not speak to them, but she managed, by peeping round the screen, to see what he was doing.

He was taking off his coat and waistcoat and putting them down behind a chair.

He added his shoes and socks.

She wondered what was happening until she saw him pull a long white silk nightshirt over his head.

He then got into the bed. Erlina saw he was holding in his hand a black bandage like the one the Marquis was wearing.

Now Erlina thought she was beginning to understand what the Marquis was planning.

As Hignet blew out the candles beside the bed, the Marquis felt for her hand.

She slipped her fingers into his, and he knew that once again she was trembling.

"It is all right," he said in a whisper. "The point is we have to catch Oliver actually attempting to murder me. That is the only way I can prevent him from trying again."

Erlina felt he could not be sure of that.

At the same time, she knew it was a mistake to question what the Marquis was doing.

She only held on to him, feeling as if his strength sustained her although she was still terribly afraid.

"I wish I had a gun," Gerry whispered.

"I am sure what the Marquis is planning is better," Erlina replied.

She hoped it was, but there was nothing she could do except pray, with her heart and soul, that nothing would go wrong.

It seemed as if a century passed as they sat in the darkness.

Then there was a slight creaking sound at the other end of the room.

Erlina knew that somebody was coming in through the door, and that it was Oliver Mell.

As he did so, Hignet began to snore loudly.

It was the snore that a drunken man might give and, Erlina thought, very convincing.

She could not see him, but she was aware that Oliver was walking slowly, as if he was not sure of his way, down the centre of the room.

He reached the window that was just beside them, and with a single movement with both of his hands pulled back the curtains.

He then unfastened the casement, pushing it wide open.

Watching from the corner where they were hiding, Erlina could hardly breathe.

If he turned and saw them, he would know that

he was not alone with his victim.

The Marquis's fingers tightened on hers and she knew he was thinking the same thing.

Now that the window was open, there was a faint light from the stars and a half moon that was creeping up the sky.

Its silver light entering the room made it easier for Oliver Mell to turn round, and walk back to the bed.

Erlina knew he would now be bending over Hignet, who continued to snore loudly.

She was aware, though she could not really see, that Oliver Mell was pulling the Valet out of bed.

He could not carry him across the room, but laid him on the floor.

Then he dragged him, moving backwards over the carpet towards the window.

It made very little sound, just the rustle of the silk nightshirt, and Oliver Mell's footsteps.

He reached the window. Hignet's face and head were obscured by the shadow his body cast with the moonlight behind him.

He paused for a moment, then bent forward.

It was then that the Marquis rose from his chair.

"Oliver!" he announced in a loud and authoritative voice. "I accuse you of attempted murder, and I have three witnesses here to prove that you are trying to kill me!"

His voice rang out.

At the first sound of it, Oliver Mell started violently, taking his hands from underneath Hignet's shoulders.

As he turned sharply to stare wildly in the direction of the voice, Oliver Mell somehow slipped on the polished floor between the carpet and the wall.

He gave a startled cry as he fell backwards over the low window-sill.

One moment he was there, the next he had disappeared.

Erlina could hardly believe it had happened.

Then, as she stared at the open window, she heard the Marquis say:

"My God! I can see! I can see!"

She looked up at him.

He was standing as he had when he accused his Cousin of attempted murder, but the bandage was no longer over his eyes.

Now he was holding it in his hand and looking at Hignet sitting up on the floor in the moonlight.

Because it was all so dramatic, and at the same time so overwhelming, Erlina felt as if everything were whirling around her, and she must faint.

For perhaps a second or two, she was almost unconscious.

Then she was aware that Gerry was jumping up and down.

Hignet was on his feet, and the Marquis was still standing with his black bandage in his hand.

In his usual respectful tone Hignet said:

"I'd better go an' tell them below, M'Lord, that while Mr. Oliver was biddin' Your Lordship good-night, 'e inadvertently fell outa th' winder."

"Send some of the men to attend to him," the

Marquis said, "and thank you, Hignet. I am very grateful."

"I will go with you," Gerry said as Hignet walked down the room.

"You do that," Hignet said, "an' I think Mrs. Dawes'll find yer a big cup o' hot choc'late. We both of us needs a drink after wot's 'appened."

He picked up his clothes and shoes from behind the chair.

A minute later Erlina heard the door shut behind them.

She felt too overcome to move.

The Marquis turned and, putting out his hand, drew her to her feet.

"H-how can you have been . . . so clever?" she managed to ask as she stood beside him. "Can . . . you . . . really see?"

The moonlight was on her face, and the Marquis said:

"You look exactly as I knew you would!"

"How . . . could you . . . know?" she murmured.

"I was looking with my heart," he answered, "and now I can do what I have been longing to do for a long time."

He pulled her into his arms, and held her close.

Then, before she could realise what was happening, his lips were on hers.

As he kissed her she knew this was what she had been longing for.

Her love was surging through her in a tidal wave.

With the moonlight silhouetting the Marquis's head, she felt as if he wore a halo like an

Archangel who had come down from Heaven.

He kissed her, at first gently, then demandingly, possessively, passionately.

He held her very close. She felt as if her whole body melted into his.

Only when he raised his head did she manage to say:

"I . . . love you . . . I . . . love . . . you."

"You told me so when you were playing to me," he said, "and I loved you for a long time before that."

"I . . . I cannot . . . believe it," Erlina whispered.

"I can hardly believe it either. But we have won the battle, and now we can live happily ever after."

She looked at him in a bewildered fashion and he said:

"I am asking you to marry me, my Darling."

"I . . . I thought you . . . said you would . . . never marry."

"What I meant was that I would never marry anyone but you," he answered. "But I thought it impossible for you to exist—and yet you do."

He kissed her again.

She felt the room was swinging round them, and they were flying into the sky.

Only when she thought it was impossible to feel such ecstasy and not die of the wonder of it, the Marquis said:

"We will be married first thing in the morning, before it is announced that Oliver is dead. I cannot wait any longer."

"H-how can you . . . do that?" Erlina asked.

"Easily," he answered. "The Vicar will marry

us. Once we are married we can be together and I shall not lie awake at night, longing to kiss you."

"Have you . . . done . . . that?"

"Every night," he answered. "Now I can have you beside me, my Darling, in my arms, and of course in my heart, as you are already."

"I . . . never dreamt you . . . l-loved me," Erlina said. "I hoped I was . . . useful . . . but . . . how could I . . . ever know that you would . . . want me as your . . . w-wife?"

"I was determined never to marry until I met you," the Marquis said.

Erlina hid her face against his neck.

"I was . . . going to . . . try to . . . persuade you to marry s-somebody in . . . order to . . . have a . . . son."

"We will have half-a-dozen sons," he said, "and they will all be as brave and sensible as Gerry."

His arms tightened as he said:

"We have so much to do together, in this house and on the Estate, besides the other places I own. I will also think of a way to restore your house, so that when the sixth Baronet wants to be married he has somewhere to live."

Erlina gave a cry.

"Only . . . you could . . . think like . . . that," she said. "Only . . . you would be . . . so kind . . . so wonderful to Gerry and me. Tell me . . . I am not . . . dreaming. Tell me . . . we will . . . never wake up."

The Marquis looked down at her.

Now, as the moonlight grew stronger, he thought no one could look more beautiful.

No woman had ever looked more radiant with the ecstasy of love.

"I love you and I worship you," he said. "This is the beginning, my Precious, of a new life. You must help me never to hurt people again."

"I know . . . now that . . . you did not . . . realise what . . . you were doing," Erlina murmured.

"We will make what reparation we can, you and I," the Marquis said, "and we will make this house a happy home for ourselves, our children, and anybody else who stays in it."

"That is . . . what I want . . . that is what I have always wanted," Erlina said, "but I am afraid . . . you may be . . . bored."

"How could I ever be bored with you?" the Marquis demanded. "And doubtless you will tell me what to do, not only with words, but with your music and, of course, with your heart."

"I will . . . do that . . . you know I will do it!" Erlina answered. "Oh, Darling Michael, I love you . . . I love you, and there are no other words in which to . . . tell you how . . . wonderful it is that, thanks to God . . . your eyes are . . . healed."

"Thanks to God—and to you!" the Marquis said as he smiled. "And that, my precious wife-to-be, is the Magic of Love!"

Then he was kissing Erlina again.

She knew as they touched the stars that their love, like the light which had healed his eyes, had come from God.

It would protect, guide, and inspire them now, and for all Eternity.

ABOUT THE AUTHOR

Barbara Cartland, the world's most famous romantic novelist, who is also an historian, playwright, lecturer, political speaker and television personality, has now written over 590 books and sold over six hundred and twenty million copies all over the world.

She has also had many historical works published and has written four autobiographies as well as the biographies of her mother and that of her brother, Ronald Cartland, who was the first Member of Parliament to be killed in the last war. This book has a preface by Sir Winston Churchill and has just been republished with an introduction by Sir Arthur Bryant.

Love at the Helm, a novel written with the help and inspiration of the late Earl Mountbatten of Burma, Great Uncle of His Royal Highness, The

Prince of Wales, is being sold for the Mountbatten Memorial Trust.

She has broken the world record for the last sixteen years by writing an average of twenty-three books a year. In the *Guinness Book of World Records* she is listed as the world's top-selling author.

Miss Cartland in 1987 sang an Album of Love Songs with the Royal Philharmonic Orchestra.

In private life Barbara Cartland, who is a Dame of the Order of St. John of Jerusalem and Chairman of the St. John Council in Hertfordshire, has fought for better conditions and salaries for Midwives and Nurses.

She championed the cause for the Elderly in 1956, invoking a Government Enquiry into the "Housing Condition of Old People."

In 1962 she had the Law of England changed so that Local Authorities had to provide camps for their own Gypsies. This has meant that since then thousands and thousands of Gypsy children have been able to go to School, which they had never been able to do in the past, as their caravans were moved every twenty-four hours by the Police.

There are now fifteen camps in Hertfordshire and Barbara Cartland has her own Romany Gypsy Camp called "Barbaraville" by the Gypsies.

Her designs "Decorating with Love" are being sold all over the U.S.A. and the National Home Fashions League made her, in 1981, "Woman of Achievement."

She is unique in that she was one and two in the Dalton list of Best Sellers, and one week had four books in the top twenty.

Barbara Cartland's book *Getting Older, Growing Younger* has been published in Great Britain and the U.S.A. and her fifth cookery book, *The Romance of Food,* is now being used by the House of Commons.

In 1984 she received at Kennedy Airport America's Bishop Wright Air Industry Award for her contribution to the development of aviation. In 1931 she and two R.A.F. Officers thought of, and carried, the first aeroplane-towed glider airmail.

During the War she was Chief Lady Welfare Officer in Bedfordshire, looking after 20,000 Servicemen and -women. She thought of having a pool of Wedding Dresses at the War Office so a Service Bride could hire a gown for the day.

She bought 1,000 gowns without coupons for the A.T.S., the W.A.A.F's and the W.R.E.N.S. In 1945 Barbara Cartland received the Certificate of Merit from Eastern Command.

In 1964 Barbara Cartland founded the National Association for Health of which she is the President, as a front for all the Health Stores and for any product made as alternative medicine.

This is now a £65 million turnover a year, with one-third going in export.

In January 1968 she received *La Médeille de Vermeil de la Ville de Paris.* This is the highest award to be given in France by the City of Paris. She has sold 30 million books in France.

In March 1988 Barbara Cartland was asked by the Indian Government to open their Health Resort outside Delhi. This is almost the largest

Health Resort in the world.

Barbara Cartland was received with great enthusiasm by her fans, who fêted her at a reception in the City, and she received the gift of an embossed plate from the Government.

Barbara Cartland was made a Dame of the Order of the British Empire in the 1991 New Year's Honours List by Her Majesty, The Queen, for her contribution to Literature and also for her years of work for the community.

Dame Barbara has now written 590 books, the greatest number by a British author, passing the 564 books written by John Creasey.

AWARDS

1945 Received Certificate of Merit, Eastern Command, for being Welfare Officer to 5,000 troops in Bedfordshire.

1953 Made a Commander of the Order of St. John of Jerusalem. Invested by H.R.H. The Duke of Gloucester at Buckingham Palace.

1972 Invested as Dame of Grace of the Order of St. John in London by The Lord Prior, Lord Cacia.

1981 Received "Achiever of the Year" from the National Home Furnishing Association in Colorado Springs, U.S.A., for her designs for wallpaper and fabrics.

1984 Received Bishop Wright Air Industry Award at Kennedy Airport, for inventing the aeroplane-towed Glider.

1988 Received from Monsieur Chirac, The Prime Minister, The Gold Medal of the City of Paris, at the Hotel de la Ville, Paris, for selling 25 million books and giving a lot of employment.

1991 Invested as Dame of the Order of The British Empire, by H.M. The Queen at Buckingham Palace for her contribution to Literature.